Sara and the Crying Clown

Anna Sellberg

Sara and the Crying Clown

Copyright © Anna Sellberg 2006
Original title: Sara och clownen som grät
Cover layout: Stabenfeldt A/S
Typeset by Roberta L. Melzl
Translated by Jeannie M. Hamrin
Published by PONY, Stabenfeldt A/S
Edited by Bobbie Chase
Printed in Germany, 2006
ISBN: 1-933343-15-X

Stabenfeldt, Inc.
457 North Main Street
Danbury, CT 06811
www.pony.us

Chapter 1

It's pitch black in the circus tent. Just a single spotlight shines on the golden sawdust. Suddenly the circus orchestra plays a little melody. But what is it? The music is in a sorrowful tempo … Umpa-umpa-umpa … tooot! In the passageway a clown with a faltering step and a sad appearance suddenly appears. Even the flower in his buttonhole is wilted. A beautiful little horse with a long white mane and a tail that trails in the sawdust follows him. She too looks sorrowful – she hangs her head, and seems to be lame in three of her four legs.

When the clown sees all the children in the audience, he suddenly changes his expression. He takes off his hat and magically pulls out a white dove that flies up to the circus tent's ceiling. The children in the audience cheer, and the little pony jumps and frolics around. The clown does several somersaults in a row and the crowd applauds. The little pony suddenly tires and lies down in front of the clown with her head raised. The clown nods and takes out a pink blow-up pillow from the pocket of his large jacket. He blows up the pillow and places it under the pony's head and she lies her head on it. He lies down beside her with his head on the pony's round stomach and snores loudly … All the children laugh and all the spotlights except for one are turned off as the orchestra plays a quiet lullaby for the clown and his little horse …

"She certainly is enchanting, huh?" said grandpa's wife Angela as she turned off the video with the remote control.

"Too small," muttered Dad reaching for the cookie plate. "What in the world would you use her for?"

"To have a foal!" said Angela with joy. "Sunshine is finished with the circus scene. Now she can come home to us, have beautiful foals, and have a good life."

I thought about the muddy, chubby little pony we had admired out in the paddock a few minutes ago. It had been raining the whole day and all of Angela's Shetland ponies loved rolling in the huge mud puddle. They looked like wandering mud figures, and the beautiful Sunshine certainly wasn't going to miss out on the fun. Her mane was no longer shiny white, but horribly gray and filled with burrs and dreadlocks. Grandpa had cut off her long white tail right below her round hocks a few days before.

"But why did the circus sell her?" I asked while I sipped my soda.

While she put the videocassette in its jacket, Angela said, "They didn't have any use for her any more."

"Even though she's so enormously clever?" asked Mom.

"Yes, but she can't take the circus life any more. She

broke a front leg a few years ago when a truck she was riding in drove into a ditch. The guy who was driving fell asleep, and … it was a terrible accident and many of the other horses died," said Angela putting the cassette on the shelf again.

"Have more coffee," she said, offering the pot to Dad who made a no thank you motion with his hand.

"No thank you, not just now," he said, and took a sugar cookie instead.

Angela was a master cookie baker. The cake plate, which was filled earlier with a good variety, was almost empty, since Dad, Mom, my little sister Sophia, and I had devoured them like a swarm of grasshoppers demolishing a field. I felt very full and would have loved to relax by lying on my back with my bare stomach facing the sun and sleeping a bit. Sophia poured more soda in her glass and smiled at Angela.

"Anyway, I think Sunshine is very sweet," she said as she flipped her long blonde hair away from her face. "I'd like to have a little horse like that at home!"

"Forget it," growled Dad. "Take care of the pony you have!"

Sophia sighed deeply and rolled her eyes, and I knew that she thought Dad had said something hopelessly dumb.

The truth is that Sophia – who is two years younger than I – fourteen years old – took over my old show pony named Camigo, but she isn't the least bit interested in horses now. She's tall and very pretty with thick, blonde hair, and she only cares about boys, make-up and music. I, on the other hand, am kind of short, have medium length blonde hair that never sits as it should, and I prefer to go around dressed in jeans and a sweatshirt. Of course sometimes I dress up, but it's obvious that you can't have a miniskirt and high heels in a stable!

It has been ages since Sophia last set foot in the stable. Camigo just hangs out in the corral and eats what he wants and gets fatter and fatter ... in reality, he's a fearless and clever show pony that Sophia could have a lot of fun with.

Sophia and I live with our parents on a farm about 15 miles outside of town. I love horses – and I love living in the country. It's wonderful for me to wake up every morning and look out my window and see the horses grazing in the sunshine. But for Sophia, country life is rank misery. She wants to move to town as quickly as she can, and later she wants to live in a city – like Chicago or New York – and work as a journalist or in the fashion field, or run a café.

As luck would have it, my boyfriend Mike is exactly like me – equally horse crazy. He works as a stable hand on our neighbors Hans and Maggie's farm. They raise Swedish warmbloods, and Mike has worked there since the spring.

It was through horses that Mike and I met, and we've been together now for almost three months. Do I need to say that these are the best three months of my life?! Mike is everything that I could dream of and we have a lot of fun together. We have the same interests and he's nice and cool and fun and ...

"Well, what do you think, Sara?" asked Angela, and I suddenly awoke from my daydream. " Is it a deal?"

"Is what a deal? I asked.

"She was thinking about Mike again," said Sophia sarcastically and elbowed me in the side. "Should we or should we not?"

"Should we what?" I said, still a bit confused.

"Stay over here next weekend," Mom interjected. "Grandpa and Angela are going away to a Shetland pony exhibition and they need someone to look after the horses while they're gone."

"I don't know," I said doubtfully. "It's almost time for the horse shows, and I have to ride each and every day."

"Alexandra and I can stay here by ourselves," suggested Sophia happily.

"Never!" shouted Mom. "Not a chance!"

Sophia gave Mom a pouty, disagreeable look, but both she and I knew what Mom was referring to – early last spring Sophia and her best friend Alexandra stayed at Alexandra's parents' house while her parents were away. They had invited a few friends over for a small get together, but the news that the parents were gone spread quickly and soon there was a ton of uninvited people. The party ended in a big fight between some hip hoppers, a punk rocker and two teenage guys from Sophia's class. The neighbors had called the police to stop the disturbance, and the police took several of the guys to the station to sober up. Two girls who weren't invited to the party were found the next day sleeping in the sauna, someone had thrown up in the shower, and the kitchen trash basket was full of cigarette butts. Besides, Alexandra's parents' expensive Oriental rug and three fine crystal pieces were ruined. They were incredibly angry and Mom and Dad had to pay for half of the cleaning bill for the rug, as well as some other things.

"Hm-mmmmm," pondered Angela. "I have no idea who else I can ask if you can't do it. Maybe we'll have to stay home from the exhibition."

"What's this nonsense?" Grandpa said sharply and looked at Sophia and me with piercing eyes. "Of *course* you'll help us!"

"Well, okay …" said Sophia slowly.

"Yes, but …" I began, but didn't complete the sentence. When grandpa sounds like that, there isn't any way to even try to discuss anything with him.

"Then we'll drive the girls here Friday afternoon," Mom said. "That's a good time, right?"

"Can Alexandra stay too?" asked Sophia, and I stared my evil look at her. I didn't have one bit of desire to be alone with those two the whole weekend. Sophia alone was bad enough – Alexandra on top of Sophia was just too much! But before I could protest, Angela said, "Of course, bring friends!" Angrily I took a gulp of my drink.

"But if Sophia can have Alexandra with her, I want Fandango," I said, referring to my roan color show pony.

"It won't work," said Dad. "The horse trailer is in the shop this whole week."

"But I have to ride!" I protested. "We're competing the weekend after this."

"Fandango won't die without a few days of training," said mother with certainty. "Now we must be getting home – it's late."

I got up and helped Angela take everything to the kitchen. A moment later we went out to the car. I looked quickly at the clock. It was 4:30, and I knew that if I wanted to ride I'd have to do it as soon as I got home. At 7:30 Mike and I were going to the movies in town.

"Mom, will you go by Alexandra's and let me off there?" asked Sophia. Mom sighed.

"Shouldn't you come home instead? You have chores to do."

"What chores?" asked Sophia, trying to look like she didn't understand.

"It's your turn to vacuum and clean the bathroom and toilet," said mother. "Besides, your room looks like a bomb fell on it."

"Why do you care? It's *my* room! And the toilet and the other chores can wait until later tonight."

"Don't try it," I said. "You're just saying that to get out of doing it."

"I am not!" hissed Sophia and drove a sharp elbow in my side.

"Ouch!" I yelled and gave her the same as payback.

"Sit still and stop fighting!" shouted Dad, who sat in the passenger seat as Mom drove. "You two are always arguing."

"Besides, I will not have Alexandra come with us to Grandpa and Angela's," I said angrily. "If Alexandra is coming, I'm staying home."

"Why don't you invite Mike over for an afternoon?" suggested Dad.

11

"He'll be away for the weekend," I replied. He and Hans are going upstate to look at a brood mare."

"That's too bad," said Dad, and I felt that he was really trying to sound as if he truly meant it. But the truth is that neither my dad nor Hans are happy that Mike and I are friends, even if it means that we can all hang out with Hans and Maggie again. Dad and Hans had a disagreement years ago over some trees that were on a wooded hill. Dad said they were his trees and Hans said they were his. Finally they agreed to have an old man come out and measure the entire area, and he found that there was almost the exact amount of trees belonging to each farm!

A short time later we turned onto the little road that led to our farm. I was looking out the window in a dream-like trance. The fields were full of ripe wheat, ready to harvest. A long way off, I saw a large red thresher that was carefully going over the field – it was one of our neighbors who had already begun to reap the harvest.

August's sunrays threw long shadows, and with a sorrowful heart I knew that summer was almost over. I wasn't happy that it was almost autumn and a new school year. I was transferring to the high school in town, and would have to take a bus in the morning and afternoon. It would mean long days with even less time for horses than I had last year. I didn't want summer to end – I wanted it to go on forever!

Mom parked the car and I got out, still in my own thoughts.

"Are you going riding?" asked Dad.

I nodded and said, "Yes. I think I'll ride out and gallop on the sand road …"

"You should ride dressage," Dad said sternly, and I knew I was about to get a lecture on how important dressage is for a show horse.

"But it's so hot," I protested. "Besides, I did dressage yesterday."

"Really? asked Dad raising an eyebrow.

"No, okay, it was the day before," I said shrugging my shoulders.

"I think you really need to train more in dressage with Fandango, and then maybe you won't come in last in dressage the next time you compete," Sophia, the brat, said. At that moment I felt that it would be so easy for me to murder her if she were just a tad closer.

"Stay out of this!" I said with a snarl." You don't ride at all any more, so you don't know what I do."

"That's true," said Sophia. "I was smart enough to stop riding! That's what separates us smart folk from you dumb folk. Anyway, can I go over to Alexandra's when I finish cleaning?"

Mom sighed, but then nodded.

"Okay, but don't forget your room."

"I won't," said Sophia as she disappeared into the house.

"If you tack up Fandango, I'll help you with dressage for a half hour," Dad said, and I knew that he thought that was a wonderful invitation.

"But …" I began, but Dad was not going to change his mind.

"If you want to compete, you have to train; it's that simple."

"You ought to be thankful that Dad wants to help you. Don't be so grumpy," said Mom as she looked at me with a wrinkled forehead. I knew she thought I was being ungrateful.

I made a face and went carefully up the porch stairs. It didn't seem as if I'd be able to get away from dressage training. Just take the bull by the horns and train a little dressage. In a way, Dad was right … it had been quite a while since Fandango and I rode dressage. But how could I get Fandango to go with me to Grandpa and Angela's farm? It was only eighteen miles there; eighteen measly miles, and yet it seemed so far with no horse trailer. Suddenly I had a great idea – I would just *ride* Fandango there!

Chapter 2

"You're not thinking about riding there, are you? Where did you get *that* crazy idea?" Dad looked at me in disbelief. "It's eighteen miles!"

"Eighteen miles is no problem for Fandango," I said calmly. "Riders who compete in long distance races often ride longer than that in one day. Besides, he's in great shape."

We sat and drank lemonade out on the lawn. Mike and I had decided not to go to town, and instead we biked down to the lake and took a dip. It had been a truly golden day – warm and cloud-free, and the lake was as still as a mirror. I was thoroughly sweaty after my dressage workout and was sure I'd have sore muscles for the next few days. Dad was satisfied with his contribution to the workout, and during dinner he babbled on and on about the training we'd done.

"I think that sounds like a reasonable idea," Mom said and Mike nodded in agreement.

"You can take the cell phone, and if something happens you can easily call for help," Mike said.

"Of course, absolutely!" I agreed.

"Which way will you ride?" Dad asked skeptically. "The highway's out because of the traffic." I knew that Dad was still uncertain about my trip.

"I'll ride the usual way through the woods, and then I'll ride across the nature preserve …" I said.

"Are you allowed to do that?" Mike interrupted, and I nodded my head and continued.

"I know the wonderful riding trails there! After the camping site by the lake, I'll take the gravel road to the little stone church. Then I have to go on the asphalt road a short way, ride across the highway at the big bridge, and after the bridge – there's just a mile or two left."

"Hmmm," Mom said, "it doesn't sound too dangerous."

"I'll start early in the morning," I said confidently. "If I ride out from here around seven, I'll be able to rest several times during the day. Besides, I'll have my cell phone and can call if something happens."

Mom and Dad looked at each other and Mom nodded her agreement.

"I think it sounds like a fine plan," she said. "I'm sure we have an old saddle bag in the attic. You can polish it up, and take your lunch and snacks in it."

"Cool! It's so tiring to ride with a backpack."

"Who's riding where with a backpack?" Sophia asked. She'd just come in after biking home from Alexandra's and overheard the last piece.

"I'm going to ride Fandango to Granddad's on Thursday," I said.

16

"Wow, that's a long ride, but how exciting! I want to ride along!" Sophia said loudly as she snatched a cherry tomato and sank down in the empty chair.

"Not in my lifetime," I said.

"No way, Camigo's not in any condition for a long ride," Dad said and he shuddered thinking about the possibility of that in his head. "We'll drive you and Alexandra to Granddad's on Friday, exactly as we decided before."

"Bummer, no fair!" Sophia whined. "Why does Sara always get to do all the fun stuff? First, she got to go to England, and now she gets to take a long trek with her horse. It's not fair!"

Mom and Dad sighed in unison but I couldn't help an inward feeling of "Nyah, nyah – I told you so." If she had worked with Camigo during the summer, he would have been in condition to take on a long ride. But now, after he had been grazing without much exercise for two months, he was as fat as our traditional Christmas pig, and there was no chance that he would make it. To get him in shape would take months and demand a lot of work.

"Sara's getting a new horse! What about me? What do I get? Nothing! I wasn't even allowed to buy new shoes when I went to a party last weekend!" continued Sophia angrily.

"Calm down now," Mom said in a firm voice. Sophia pressed her lips tightly together while sending me a hateful look.

"You're forgetting something," I said. "Winny isn't a gift – I paid for her myself."

"Really," said Sophia with raised eyebrows. "You can afford a horse? With what money?"

"I took all the returnable bottles that you and Alexandra just threw in the old stable," I teased as Sophia gasped and then let out an exaggerated breath.

"What? I...I don't know what you're talking about!" She pretended not to know what I meant and suddenly got out of her chair and went into the house.

"I don't understand what's going on with her," Dad said shaking his head. "She's becoming worse every day."

"Teens are like that," Mom reassured him as she put her hand on his. "Just try to wait her out, and she'll come around."

"Hmmm." Dad said. I knew that he didn't agree.

It was getting late and time for Mike to go home. Our black lab, Swift, and I walked with him. We held hands as we walked along in the darkening August night and I thought about how lucky I was to have found such a great guy.

When we reached Hans and Maggie's farm, we kissed good night. Mom and Dad were already in bed when I got home. I could see Camigo and Dad's old competition horse, Maverick, standing half asleep in the moonlight. Fandango was in the stable since we're competing in a couple of weeks and he has to keep his weight down. He wasn't exactly happy when I put him in his box stall for the night. On the other hand, I knew that he loved to lie down and sleep in the soft straw. I quietly crept into the stable and looked in Fandango's stall. He was already sleeping on his side, stretched out like a large gray walrus. He didn't bother to get up when I came over. He just lay there and lifted his head a bit in acknowledgement, and then he lay it down again and went back to sleep.

I laughed inside as Swift and I went into the house and I got in my cool, soft bed. I was really tired, as it had been a long day, and all the cookies still sat in a lump in my stomach. That night I dreamed about clowns, small fat ponies and cookies. I couldn't remember exactly what the dream was about the next morning – only that something unpleasant had happened, and that I blamed myself for eating too many cookies.

About mid morning, Mike and I went for a ride together. He rode Hans and Maggie's stallion named Fireflight and I, of course, rode Fandango. Copying Mike's stirrups, I hoisted up Fandango's a few notches, and while we were galloping along a soft sand trail in the woods I pretended that I was a famous jockey on a world-renowned steeplechase horse – only Fandango didn't have the slightest chance against the long legged, fast and drop-dead handsome Fireflight. He tried to go faster, and suddenly we were only twenty yards behind even though Fandango was moving like a powerful steam engine. Fandango was no match for Fireflight, who had been a top racehorse with several important wins in races for two and three-year-olds. Now that he was older, he was Hans and Maggie's stud horse, and I secretly dreamed about breeding Winny with Fireflight next year. It would be one unbelievable foal!

When we arrived home, both horses were sweaty and Fireflight shook his head to get rid of all the flies. Fandango had his anti-fly band with long strands on his brow band and was at least free from this irritation. Hans thought that things like anti-fly bands were just a sham, but I knew that Mike didn't always agree with his boss.

When I came into our yard, Mom was outside spraying the rose bed with an insecticide. The sun had dipped behind a cloud and the air was oppressively close which made me think I might get a headache at any moment.

"Jessie called a couple of hours ago," Mom called to me. "Winny was vetted and she's fine and ready to go."

"Hooray," I cheered and slid off Fandango, who began to rub his big head against me. "Then she's coming soon, or –?"

"I think so, but give Jessie a call," said Mom. "She'll also e-mail you, even though I warned her that we were having problems with our modem lately."

I hurriedly took Fandango to the stable, and while I un-saddled and unbridled him, my thoughts were elsewhere. I smiled lovingly when I thought about Winny, a beautiful brown mare with an elegant velvet-soft mane and a white star on her forehead. She is the horse of my dreams. I thought back to my vacation in England and how I had managed to borrow her from Fiona, my best friend Jessie's friend. I showed her, and later was invited to buy the fantastic horse.

And soon she'll be here and she'll belong to me! I'm sure she'll step out of the horse transport like a queen with her beautiful head high, the small pointed ears and the large sparkling brown eyes full of the joy of being alive. My feelings for her are entirely different from what I feel for Fandango … not stronger or more – but just different!

I dragged the hose around and rinsed Fandango. He loved this and nickered his enjoyment as the warm water ran over him. His dapple-gray roan color was still relatively dark in spite of his being eleven years old. Fandango is muscular and almost 15 hands at the withers. I had him since he was a colt, but soon our time together would end. I felt sad as I let him out with the other horses in the field and saw him lie down and roll in the dustiest spot he could find. He was satisfied and happy that his immediate needs had been met, and didn't have any idea about what the future had in store. I was 16 years old and wouldn't want a show horse for more than two more years. And I knew what would happen then – Dad was already talking about selling Fandango. It was one thing for Camigo to go around the pasture doing nothing but grazing. He was old and had been in the family for years. Fandango was different – he was a show pony. He loved to jump and gallop out on the trails. To put him out to pasture and just have him for a few walking rides every now and then was unthinkable.

I took the telephone to my room, and lifted the receiver to dial Jessie's number. The line was dead! I punched numbers on the pad and it had absolutely no effect, so I placed the receiver back in the holder. Mom had come in and was in the kitchen mixing more insecticide for the roses. I asked her what was wrong with the phone.

"Is there something wrong with it? Jessie just called you a few hours ago, so it was working then," she said with surprise. "How strange!"

At that moment, Sophia came into the kitchen.

"Alexandra and I are leaving to take a swim now. Later on we're going to a cookout with some friends at the campsite."

"Don't come home too late!" Mom warned. "Don't forget your cell phone, and promise that you won't go with anyone to some other place."

"No," said Sophia reassuringly and she made a dismissing gesture with her hand. "We can take care of ourselves, I promise!"

"Anyway, do you know what's wrong with the phone?" I said and Sophia's face looked like a living question mark.

"Wrong? No idea," she said quickly, and then hurriedly left, banging the door.

"I'll call the phone company and see if it's a downed line," Mom said and went to get her cell phone. We sometimes get broken lines out here in the country.

I went upstairs to take a quick shower. I was thoroughly sweaty after our ride and looked forward to the warm water soothing my aching muscles from the dressage practice the evening before.

I had just dressed myself and was on my way downstairs when I heard Mom's angry voice from the kitchen. When I entered the kitchen she was talking on the cell phone. She was really angry! Not just a little angry, but super explosive angry! And she was angry with Sophia!

"You come home at once. There will be no party for you tonight because Dad and I need an explanation. That means right now this minute! I will pick you up in five minutes. You had better be ready to go. No excuses. You are coming home *immediately*!"

Mom turned off the cell phone and I carefully asked why she was so upset.

"The phone's not broken," she said angrily. "It's shut off! The bill hasn't been paid."

"What?" I said with surprise, as I knew how careful Mom was with paying bills on time.

"First, I haven't received a bill! Someone has taken both the bill and the reminder that was sent, apparently to hide from me that the bill was so high."

Mom snatched her pocketbook, which was hanging from one of the kitchen chairs.

"The telephone bill is almost a thousand dollars!" she said furiously as she marched out the door. "It's Sophia's internet chats that account for the largest part. But as of now, that's stopped!"

She went out of the house and slammed the door. I couldn't help but feel a little sorry for Sophia – but I was also really glad that I wasn't the target of Mom's anger!

Chapter 3

I woke up early the next morning. The sun was shining through my thin flowery curtains and the whole house was absolutely still. The calmness was just wonderful – I guessed that Mom and Dad were still furious with Sophia since I'd heard what sounded like World War III the night before.

It was because Sophia liked to enter chat rooms, and at the start of summer she practically sat at the computer all day and all night. Mom and Dad have a pay by the minute plan, so every minute on the Internet costs money, and Sophia had just stayed connected hour after hour. She did it more at night, so it was understandable that Mom and Dad hadn't noticed that the telephone was always busy.

Anyway, the day the phone bill arrived in the mailbox, Sophia had made a stupid mistake and removed the bill before Mom discovered it. When Sophia saw how much it was, she went into a panic mode and suddenly lost all memory, and for the whole time she was in chat rooms she just pretended that she wasn't there!

"But I don't understand! Why?" Dad asked the night before as he pulled at his hair when he and Mom were talking calmly in between scolding Sophia about what she had done.

"Didn't you know that we'd find out sooner or later?" Mom asked, and Sophia just shook her head.

"I'd planned on paying it myself," she said with tears in her eyes. "I tried to get a summer job at hundreds of places just to pay it off! But no one would hire me, and then … I was too scared to tell you!"

I must admit that I felt genuinely sorry for Sophia. Dad and Mom are really nice and calm most of the time, but when they're angry – firestorms erupt. Strange as it seems, they're less angry about the phone bill than they are about Sophia hiding it from them.

I got out of bed, stretching my mouth into a huge yawn. Riding pants and a pretty cotton shirt were laid out and I hopped into them, combed my hair and crept quietly downstairs. Swift was sleeping in the hallway as usual, and he didn't even lift his head as I tiptoed by.

Fandango seemed just as sleepy as Swift, but at least he got up. I brushed and combed his mane and tail. Then I saddled and bridled him. Mom had naturally forgotten to look for the saddlebag the night before, so I put what I needed in my backpack.

At 7:35 Fandango and I slipped quietly out of the yard. The air was already humid, but Fandango strode happily forward. He was excited and in top form, in spite of the fact that we had galloped the day before with Mike.

I shortened the reins and began to trot, eager to ride away from home, away from the old well-known trails that I had ridden at least a thousand times before. I was convinced that Fandango and I were going to have an exciting adventure!

We turned into the woods on a long soft logging road. I let Fandango gallop a little, and he pulled hard on the bit to go faster.

"Now slow down," I said and patted him on the neck, "we've got a long way to go. Save your strength for later …" It was wonderful in the woods. The sun's rays trickled though the trees' branches, and the air smelled of pine needles, warm summer earth and summer horse. I knew exactly where we were. I had ridden here many times before, but I usually turned around after a short way and rode home again along another winding path. Fandango was surprised when we kept going straight ahead.

I slowed down and let him go at his own pace with long reins. Flies buzzed all around us, so I broke off a twig from a bush to swish them away. We turned onto a gravel road, and after about two miles I saw the large Nature Reserve sign.

There were many different paths that I could take as indicated on the sign. I quickly found the main riding trail, which was fabulously springy and soft to ride on. We trotted for a while, and then I let Fandango go at his own pace again with free reins while I sat, humming happily to myself, knowing that life could never be any better than this!

At about 10:30 my stomach was suddenly complaining for food. It was time to get out the lunch packet, and after a while we came to a little picnic spot and I reined in Fandango and hopped off.

I chose the heavy wooden table that was most protected from the trail and Fandango began at once to graze. It was hot, the flies buzzed persistently around us, and every now and then a wasp – as large as a B-52 bomber – would fly by. As one approached me, I jumped up! I hate wasps. When I looked around I could understand why they loved this place. A short distance from the table there was an overflowing garbage can with the lid half-slanted off. Garbage bulged out where crows and other animals had ripped the garbage bag open to help themselves to the leftovers. Half-eaten scraps of food and soda bottles with a little bit of sugary liquid left in the bottom were all over the ground, and the wasps were attacking them with a vengeance.

"Yuck, this stinks!" I yelled to Fandango who quite naturally didn't care at all.

I jammed my crumbling sandwich and juice box in my backpack again. I definitely wasn't going to stay here – that was for sure!

We continued along the trail. Up until now we hadn't met a single person, but suddenly that changed. I heard a child shriek and laugh. Fandango raised his head curiously with his ears standing up straight, and immediately in front of us there appeared a small opening at the side of the trail. There was a mom, dad and three children between the ages of four and nine. All three were girls, and when they saw

27

Fandango the oldest one gave a joyful shout and came rushing forward to pat him.

It just so happens that my pony loves children. It almost hurts to see how he lets small kids caress him, pull on his ears, and feed him with clumps of grass they hold in their hands. The kids were absolutely ecstatic to come upon a real live horse in the middle of the woods. Even their Mom and Dad came over to make a fuss over Fandango.

We chatted a bit, and I told them about the spoiled picnic spot and all the garbage. They had already discovered it, and that was why they were picnicking in the small wood-land meadow instead.

It didn't take me long to decide that I'd rest here too. Fandango calmly began to graze, while the little girls ripped up grass for him and fed him with sugar bits, cookie pieces and apples. I started to eat my falling-apart soggy sandwich and drink my lukewarm juice.

"Oh, you poor dear," the mom said looking at my spartan and yucky unappealing lunch. "Don't you have more than that? You've got a long ride ahead."

"Nah," I said, "it's okay for me."

"You're welcome to have some chicken if you want," the dad said graciously. "We have more than enough food with us."

And so I sat down on their blanket and ate grilled chicken with potato salad and drank an ice-cold cola that had just come out of their cooler instead of my own sad lunch. While I was eating, the mom hand-led Fandango around the clearing with each child, one at a time on his back.

After lunch it was time for me to start off again.

"I want to take riding lessons this fall!" the oldest girl said in a demanding voice while I climbed up on Fandango.

"You're on the waiting list at the riding school," her mom said stroking her hair. "I hope you get in."

"And when I grow up I'm going to have a horse just like him!" the girl said, and when I saw the determined look in her eyes, I knew she would make sure it happened!

It was now noon. The sun was hot and the sky was a clear blue. Under the trees it was relatively cool, but tons of small blackflies and a few enormous horse flies droned around us. I let Fandango trot for several hundred yards hoping that would make it better. But as soon as we stopped the flies buzzed us again.

In a short while, we came to a split in the woods' path. We were now a little more than halfway and it was going much quicker than I had thought when I had looked at the map at home.

Fandango was anxious to continue and I patted his neck happily. He liked this adventure just as much as I did!

We chose the path that went to the right. It winded gently downhill, and I soon got a glimpse of blue water between the trees. That would be the lake inlet that I was familiar with, and I knew we would soon pass an area with small camps and trailers.

Just as we stepped onto the path we heard a cracking sound in the bushes behind us and Fandango came to a dead stop on the path. Before I could get him under control and moving again, he whirled around with his head high and ears erect. We were staring at a mountain biker who came out of the woods a few feet from us. The guy gave us a nonchalant disinterested look, and then took off straight over the path, disappearing amongst the trees again. Even though he was gone, Fandango was frozen to the spot, and suddenly he showed his displeasure with a loud snort.

"Okay, it's cool, take it easy," I said and patted him calmly on the neck.

At that moment I heard someone shout, "Look out!" and there was another mountain biker coming through the trees right at us!

Without even trying to slow down, he passed Fandango and me at a terrifying speed. His bike had a noisemaker fastened to the front wheel, which made a frightening sound.

My pony had definitely had enough and freaked out. He threw me sideways and I had no chance to stay seated. As luck would have it, I landed gently, almost like I had stepped down and landed on my feet. In spite of that piece of good luck, I couldn't hold the reins when Fandango quickly pulled backward, threw himself around and rushed away toward the campgrounds at a full gallop.

Fandango took off with thundering hoofs around a bend and vanished as suddenly as the bikers had – leaving me standing alone on the path. I really wasn't quite alone – as there were a million flying, biting insects to keep me company!

"Oh, no!" I screamed, and let out a long stream of words that aren't suitable to say, let alone print. Then I started to jog along the path as quickly as I could. It was easy to follow Fandango's hoof prints in the soft path, but fear sat the whole time like a hard knot in my stomach.

It was hot. The sun bore down from the cloud-free sky and I felt the sweat pour from my body. The mosquitoes and their ravenously hungry companions, the bloodsucking blackflies, *attacked* me eagerly and nonstop. I slapped at them angrily. After a while I slowed down and took off my riding helmet. I held it in my hand, swinging it as I ran at a breathless pace.

I prayed that Fandango had chosen the path to the campgrounds. I was hoping that some friendly person would be able to catch him and take care of him until I could get there. But if he went into the miles and miles of woods at the side of the road, I knew I didn't stand a chance of ever finding him.

I don't know how long I ran, but it felt like several marathons. My throat was raw from breathing so hard and I had a pain in my side. Even so, I forced myself onward. The hoof prints were still visible and it appeared that Fandango had slowed from a full gallop to a trot.

"Why can't you just stop and eat, you naughty horse," I muttered to myself. I was forced to stop and lean forward to try to get the horrible side pain to go away. With irritation I wiped the sweat from my forehead. Salty drops ran into my eyes and my back was soaking wet under my backpack.

I walked a little way and then began to half-run half-jog again. The trail sloped gently down, and there before me the woods ended, with a single path cutting through a

31

gently sloping downward meadow. At the bottom, the lake glittered in the sun and it was as peaceful and idyllic as could be. The camping spot was a few hundred yards away right on the beach. I stopped and took a couple of deep breaths before I slowly began to jog down to the trailers and tents. Fandango's hoof prints were no longer as visible, but a mountain of horse dung assured me I was on the right path. The sharp sunlight made me squint as I searched the tents, beach and trailers for a glimpse of him. Groups of children were splashing water at the shore's edge, suntanned adults were half sleeping in their lawn chairs or under umbrellas, kids were playing beach volleyball with radios cranked at high decibels, and the line at the ice cream stand was at least 20 yards long – but no Fandango. Where in the world could he have gone?

Chapter 4

Panting for breath, I came to the first cabin and found an old lady watering her pink begonias with a large watering can.

"Did you see a horse run by?"

"What?" she said as she put her hand up to her ear.

"Have you seen a gray horse?" I yelled and the old lady nodded happily.

"Yeah, I saw one!" she said. "Yesterday when my son drove me to town we drove by a pasture and there was a beautiful gray horse …"

I sighed, said good-bye and continued among the cabins. Most of them were empty – and even worse they were all empty of a large sweaty gray pony! I asked a couple of people, but no one had seen Fandango. Three horse-loving ten or eleven-year olds said they would help me look for him and gratefully I accepted their offer. We split up and searched everywhere, but neither Fandango nor any trace of him could be found.

We eventually met up at the ice cream stand and sadly acknowledged that we hadn't seen any sign of him.

Suddenly a tall dark-haired man with a long beard came along. He held a little girl by one hand and she held an ice cream cone in the other. When he caught sight of me his face lit up, and they came over to us.

"Are you the one who lost a horse?" he asked, and I nodded with hope.

"Yes, have you seen him?"

"Yes, my oldest daughter took him over to the circus. We thought that he belonged there. They have tons of horses there."

"Oh," I said. "Where's the circus?"

"Just a little bit in that direction," said the man as he made a gesture with his hand past the ice cream stand. "On the other side of the grove there's a large field where they've put up their tent."

"Great!" yelled my helpers. "Come on! Let's go!"

"But can you leave without telling your parents?" I asked doubtfully.

"Of course we can," said the smallest girl, a redhead with Pippi Longstocking pigtails. She raised her eyebrows and looked at her buddies, and I knew she thought I was some crazy adult.

"We've already been over there two times today to pet the horses. They have adorable little Shetland ponies there!" said one of the other girls. "I got to hold his reins while he was grazing!"

"Okay," I said. I thanked the man for his help, and we ran toward the circus. At last! As we turned the corner the circus tent popped into view, and I could see Fandango's gray coat shining in the sun. He was dark with sweat, and danced around a small light-haired girl who nervously held him by the absolute end of the reins. His nervousness wasn't particularly surprising – he had definitely never seen a circus tent before! Outside the tent stood two clowns, each holding a tired-looking Shetland pony. Both ponies had western saddles on their backs. A third clown tried, without success, to make order of a small line of babbling, nagging children who all wanted to ride first. Two shaggy dogs were running around loose and bouncing and playing and, a bit further away, a large man in shorts and a dirty t-shirt was trying to set up a large game with a chance wheel.

"Oh, what a beautiful horse you have!" enthused the girl holding Fandango. "He's wonderful!"

"Yes, he is," I agreed and ran forward and grabbed the reins because I saw that she was about to drop them.

"Thanks so much!" I said gratefully, and the girl looked relieved at not having to hold the reins. I quickly checked Fandango out. He seemed unhurt, and with a shaking hand I patted him on the neck.

The redheaded girl smiled while both she and my three other helpers patted Fandango where they could reach him and muttered loving words to him in soft tones. Fandango understood that he was the center of everyone's adoration, and now that he had calmed down he was enjoying all the attention.

At that moment two men came over to us. One was large and presented himself with such great authority that I knew he must be the circus director. The other man was notably younger. He had dark hair and ice-cold blue eyes.

"I guess you've found your horse?" the circus director said in a friendly tone as he shook my hand. "I was worried when no one claimed him, and was just going to call the police."

"Yeah, he's mine. His name's Fandango," I said. "I'm on my way to my Granddad and Angela's house. They live in Appleton, and I'm going there to horse sit their miniature Shetland ponies while they're away. I've got to ride over 'cuz our horse trailer's broken and …"

I was so happy to have Fandango back that I just babbled on as both the circus director and two clowns passing by grinned at me. The dark young man, however, didn't smile at all. He was looking down like he was studying his ripped white tennis shoes.

"Well, hi again," acknowledged the now broadly smiling circus director. "I know your Granddad's wife, Angela. She is his wife, right?"

"Yeah," I said, surprised, but suddenly a light bulb went on. The circus tent had the same colors as the one in Angela's video!

"So Sunshine belonged here before Angela bought her?" I asked and the circus director nodded.

"Yes, she was our little circus star. Perhaps you know that we're famous for our fine miniature Shetland ponies? Sunshine hurt herself a few years ago, and since she never recovered completely, we sold her to Angela to become a brood mare instead. We're training a new star to replace her."

36

"But there'll never be another Sunshine," interrupted the young man with the dark hair in a bitter voice. "She was the best!"

"Yes, but it's how it had to be, Marko. Things happen …"

"I know," said Marko bitterly as the circus director sighed.

I bet that these two had discussed the issue many, many times before, and Marko clearly hadn't forgiven the director for selling her.

"Well, why don't you give your horse a little water before you head out?" invited the circus director, and I nodded thankfully.

He took us to an open-sided wagon with a large tank and a tap on the short side. Underneath the tap there was a bunch of buckets. The circus director filled one of the buckets with water and Fandango drank with deep gulps while we stood and made small talk about the circus's miniature Shetland ponies and Angela's small breeding farm.

The clowns with the two tired ponies had come over, as the pony rides were finished for now. Fandango stared suspiciously at the small ponies, and when one of them reached out to playfully nip him he took a few anxious steps to the side.

I thanked the circus people for all their help and the water, and the circus director asked me to take his best wishes to Angela and Sunshine. Since he had other things to do, he disappeared among the wagons. I let Fandango graze from the short-cut grass while I took off my backpack and looked for my juice drink. The three small girls and the one that was a little older continued to pat and make a fuss over Fandango.

As soon as I had finished my drink and washed up a bit, I prepared to mount. I took out six wrinkled dollars from the outer pocket of my backpack and gave them to the girls as thanks for all their help.

They hugged Fandango one last time and then set off toward the campgrounds as quickly as their legs would take them – the ice cream stand was their goal, I guessed.

I straightened up and looked back toward the circus wagons where everyone but Marko was busy with some activity. He stood casually leaning against one of the walls with his hands jammed in his pants pockets and an angry expression on his face. Suddenly our eyes met, and he stared hatefully at me before making a quick about-face and disappearing behind a trailer. I looked after him and then quickly got up on Fandango and rode away from there as quickly as I could.

It felt incredibly peaceful when we got out to the gravel road and left the circus and the camping place far behind us. I kept thinking about Marko's mean look and how it had frightened me …

The gravel road was only a half-mile long and it ended at a lovely old church. Unfortunately the end of the gravel road now forced me to follow the asphalt county road for a few miles. It had seemed like a relatively short way on the map, but now that we were on it, it seemed unbelievably long. The sun was burning hot from the cloud-free sky, the air above the road shimmered from the heat, and there wasn't a bit of shade to be found. Along the road there was a huge wheat and rye field edged with masses of cornflowers, milkweed, and daisies.

There wasn't so much as a puff of wind, and my throat was as dry as the Sahara desert. I felt the sweat run down my back. The backpack's straps were cutting into my shoulders, and the cars were speeding by every now and then, which didn't exactly make things better. Most of them didn't care at all about Fandango and me. They just accelerated, going at top speed, some even honked at us to get out of the way. I had no idea what they expected, but I guessed they thought that my horse and I should jump off the road or get on a bus. Because Fandango is so road-wise I tried to not care about them, but it wasn't always easy.

At one point Fandango and I were really scared when a motorcyclist appeared suddenly in front of us. We were on a long stretch of road with deep ditches on both sides, and when I saw that black spot coming nearer and nearer, I quickly shortened the reins. But I hardly had time to do that when the motorcycle came roaring by us at about 90 miles per hour! Panic stricken, I pulled Fandango to the side and stopped dead at the edge of the ditch! I felt sick to my stomach, but as luck would have it, Fandango didn't jump into the ditch …

A long while after both he and I were still trembling, and I was thinking nasty thoughts about irresponsible motorcyclists who drive over the speed limit and don't stop for horses!

Pretty soon we came to a place where the old county road that we were on passed under the new super highway. The highway was raised on large pilings high above us, and I had worried about this crossing the night before. But it was no problem at all. Fandango was, at first, a little skeptical, but we soon moved quickly under the raised highway at a brisk trot. His hoofs sounded clippity, clippi-ty, clop on the road. Fandango trotted forward the whole time, while the sounds of the weekend warriors on their way home roaring by at high speed filled our ears, and soon we were on the other side and the highway was behind us. After passing the on ramp to the highway, and the high chain link fence that kept the deer and other wild animals away from the traffic, I could now steer Fandango to the right, away from the road. We could ride on the shoulder and on a large field that reached all the way to the end of the woods. It was much cooler in the woods, and I patted Fandango on his neck lovingly. There wasn't too much farther to go!

The road through the woods turned out to be blocked off by a locked gate. It was a gate that you could open if you had the key to the padlock. I walked Fandango up to it, wondering what I should do. Both sides of the road had sheep fencing, and I knew the fencing went for a long way on both sides. So, what now? Ride back to the highway, follow that a bit and then take the gravel road to Angela and Granddad's farm? That would be a huge detour, and both Fandango and I were starting to get tired. From this spot there was hardly one mile left if we could go straight through the woods. It would be at least four or five miles more if we took the detour around.

So we did the only smart thing – I let Fandango check out the height of the gate, turned him around, galloped him down the road so he was wide awake, and then turned him again and we headed for the gate at full gallop.

Fandango understood at once what I wanted him to do! With his head high and his hoofs thundering on the road we flew toward the gate. I felt in his whole body how happy he was – this was a much better way to go than walking slowly along a boring highway!

I tried to rein in Fandango a bit as we came closer to the gate as I sensed he was going too fast. But he just threw his head and grabbed the bit, and I suddenly remembered why I used to have a martingale on him when we competed. I knew that I didn't have a chance of stopping him. Instead I let him determine the tempo as I sat still in the saddle. The gate wasn't too high and I trusted my pony one hundred percent!

Three … two … one … UP! Fandango lifted up and sailed high over the gate. We landed without any problem on the other side, and I let Fandango gallop some more. He was pulling hard on the bit, and when I finally reined him in he snorted angrily and threw his head, doing a little side prance to show me he wanted to keep going. I grinned and stroked his neck. What a magnificent horse! We had been riding for several hours, it was as warm as an oven, we had several problems along the way, and he was just as happy and positive as ever. Oh, how I loved him, my teddy bear pony.

We walked the last three hundred yards to Granddad and Angela's. The air was still hot and close, the flies and other biting insects buzzed around us like crazy and, in spite of my efforts to slap at them with a leafy twig, they refused to leave us alone.

At last, the white fence was right in front of us. If you didn't know that Angela worked with Shetland ponies, you would think you were in Fairyland! Granddad and Angela's farm is entirely taken over by Shetland ponies, mostly miniatures. All the painted white wooden fences are very low. In the barn, the box stalls have walls half the normal height, and hayracks and water buckets are at knee height. It's all so super cutesy-poo that if you didn't know Angela personally it would seem kinda gross! Angela is a gray-haired, stern and rather plump woman, who always dresses in a pair of well-worn blue jeans, shapeless shirts and a baseball hat from a tractor factory that she should probably donate to a homeless person. She and Granddad are a perfect fit. He goes around in his faded blue overalls, whether it's summer or winter. The difference between summer and winter is that in winter, he usually buttons the overalls and weaves a hand-knitted scarf around his neck.

The only decent-sized horse on the whole farm is Angela's daughter's aging Fjord Horse, Buster. I knew that he had a pasture with a regular horse fence, so I decided to put Fandango in there with him. I rode into the yard and could feel Fandango getting excited. He raised his head and gazed at everything. In a pasture a little way away the whole herd of miniature Shetland ponies in all possible colors galloped to the fence to get a look at the new arrival. Fandango snorted excitedly. He had been to Granddad and Angela's farm several times before, and he was always curious about the small horses.

Angela and Granddad came out of the house. Granddad puffed as usual on his old pipe and Angela was dressed in a pair of unbecoming red shorts and an outdated black tee shirt that said "Black Sabbath" on it.

"Welcome!" she said gladly and, glancing at the clock, added, "You're so late!"

"I took it slow," I said, as I didn't have the energy to tell her everything that had happened along the way – at least not right now.

"If you want to rinse off your horse, the hose is in the barn. Tonight we'll bathe all the ponies for tomorrow's show, so there's no reason for you to shower before we've done that," continued Angela, and I made a face.

I'd hoped that she'd already bathed all the ponies, because I knew from experience that this was one horrendous job: tiny angry Shetland ponies who don't want to be shampooed, unmannerly foals that kick with one end and bite with the other, hair everywhere, and Angela's orders that I never succeed in following no matter how hard I try!

I dismounted and felt how tired I was. My muscles ached and I moved as stiffly as an old woman. I led Fandango into the barn where he was placed in Buster's stall for now. He drank several gulps of water, and then began to search for hay pieces Buster might have forgotten. Unfortunately, there weren't any! I unsaddled him and hitched him to the ties outside the stall. Fandango enjoyed a lukewarm shower, and then when I put him in the pasture he ran straight to his favorite place and rolled in the dirt.

Just as I shut the gate I heard thundering hoofs, and Buster came galloping from the grove of trees. He nickered happily to his guest. Soon the two old friends grazed side by side in the late afternoon sun. Then it was my turn to sit down and have a quick snack with Granddad and Angela before it was time to bathe and scrub the ponies for the show the next day.

Many long hours later I lay in the tub with water up to my chin. Every single muscle in my body ached. I could count three black and blue marks of different sizes, and my hands were rubbed raw trying to hold onto one of the Shetland mares that had broken loose when it was her turn to be washed.

A little tiger striped Shetland stallion with extra sharp teeth had nipped me two times, *and* kicked me hard in the shins. Two of the foals had escaped and gone under the fence into Fandango and Buster's pasture, and it was a very tough job to get them out of the pasture because both geldings wanted to adopt them.

A really sweet young mare managed to get out of her halter and gallop into the yard where she romped back and forth in the flower garden and on the lawn, so clods of dirt and plants flew everywhere. Granddad tried to drive her away with a broom, but that did no good. It wasn't until Angela's beautiful black cat Mimi ambled toward the Shetland and showed her that she was really angry that the mare went hurrying back to the pasture. The mare bravely threw herself, in a tiger-like pounce, over the fence where the others were waiting for her. Then the whole herd of ponies galloped away with her as far away as they could go – which was a good distance away! It took Angela and me over an hour to catch her again. Angela uttered lots of bad words and said that the evil beast should be sold to a riding school for young children as soon as possible! But now all the show ponies were sparkling clean and groomed. During the night they would sleep in their stalls with heavy layers of fresh hay to keep them clean for tomorrow.

I got out of the bathtub, brushed my teeth and lay down in the soft bed in the guest room. I fell asleep at once and dreamed a strange dream about Fandango turning into a miniature Shetland pony and a clown with completely black eyes trying to change him back again.

Chapter 5

I don't know what it was that woke me, but it was definitely not the alarm clock. I took a look at the clock, and it was only half past three. I could sleep in for several more hours!

The first gray dawn's light filtered through the thin curtains as I rolled over in bed and buried my head in the pillow, trying to fall back asleep.

That was when I heard the sound of many small hoofs … one horse whinnied eagerly, and suddenly I remembered that it was a whinny that woke me up a few minutes earlier!

Before I was totally awake I jumped out of bed and rushed over to the window and looked out. It wasn't Fandango out on a spree, was it?

Well, no – it wasn't. It was much worse! When I pushed the curtain aside I could see a sight from one of my worst nightmares – and I pinched myself in the arm to be sure I was really awake.

All the Shetland ponies that had been securely locked up in the barn were now loose in the courtyard!

"Oh, no!" I groaned, and I hurried to wake Granddad and Angela, but then I heard their door open with a bang. Angela ran down the stairs two at a time, shouting loudly, and then flew out the door, slamming it with so much force that the window frames shook. I shoved my feet into my sneakers, pulled on a sweater and ran after her.

Thank goodness the ponies hadn't gotten very far. Most had just stopped to eat, except for the beautiful young mare that lay down and rolled back and forth with all four legs in the air. She had a very special color – her main was black, but she had white spots (exactly like an appaloosa) over her loins and hindquarters. I knew that she would definitely have to be bathed again if she were going to the show …

Angela was able to catch the young stallion first, which made it easier to secure the others. The horses seemed surprised by what had happened, and they walked calmly into their stalls again.

When we finally had the horses secured again, Angela caught her breath and flashed angry eyes at me.

"Were you down in the stable late last night? I know you went out around ten o'clock," she said.

"No! I just went out to Fandango and Buster's pasture."

Angela looked stern, but I knew that she believed me.

"I don't understand this!" she sighed, and then clasped her hands together. How could all the horses get out at the same time? They can't exactly open their stall doors themselves!"

I tried the latch on the nearest stall door. The bolt was tightly drawn; the door felt secure, and there was no chance in the world that a pony could open it from the inside.

Angela looked around suspiciously.

"I wonder if someone's playing with me!" she said.

"Are there any teens around here who'd do this as a prank?" I replied.

Angela shook her head.

"No teens or children live around here. And it's way too far for someone from the campgrounds to come here during the day, let alone in the middle of the night."

"The only explanation is that someone let the horses out on purpose," Granddad speculated as he joined us in the stable. He had on a pair of fuzzy slippers and a pair of baggy pajama pants, and his hair stood on end.

"But who would do such a thing?" I asked. "You don't have any enemies, do you?"

Angela shook her head.

"None that I know of … I'm even friends with that old witch who's chairman of our local union – at least for now!"

"Yeah, just think!" Granddad grinned. "Angela's been dancing with the devil!"

"Well, maybe I should run through my list of friends who I think *are* friends!" Angela continued without bothering to acknowledge his sarcastic comment.

"Let's get some sleep," said Granddad.

"There's hardly any time left to try to sleep now," groaned Angela. "I have to shampoo Spotty again before we leave."

"Do you want me to help, or can I go back to bed?" I asked, and tried to conceal a big yawn.

"Go back to bed," Angela said. "I'm going to make a cup of coffee before I start. And then I'll sit out on the veranda and drink it. No one's going to sneak in here again tonight – that's for sure!"

"Do you want the shotgun?" Granddad asked, and Angela looked like she was seriously considering accepting before she finally shook her head.

"No, I can take care of anyone," she muttered. "I'm going to make coffee – any takers?"

I slept well and didn't wake up until Angela knocked on my door around eight o'clock. In the courtyard in front of the barn Granddad had driven his old refrigerator truck that he'd remodeled for transporting Shetland ponies. It was absolutely amazing inside, and there was even a small dressing room, but it made me a little envious that every-thing was made for small ponies. There was just no way it could be made big enough to accommodate Fandango, which meant we couldn't borrow it to travel to shows.

"Are you ready to go?" I asked sleepily, and Angela nodded.

"Yeah, we're ready, you sleepy head! Hope it goes well with all the horses this weekend."

"Not to worry, it will," I said and sat up in bed, moaning when I realized how much my whole body hurt, and Angela just sighed.

"The younger generation is too soft," she said. "Get up right now. Half the day's already gone!"

I nodded, wiping the sleep out of my eyes. Angela

49

walked out of the room, and I heard her stomp loudly down the stairs.

I stretched, got up and dressed. Down in the kitchen I fixed a bowl of cereal, poured myself a glass of juice, and sat at the kitchen table to look at the newspaper.

The centerfold had a huge article about the circus, with photos of performers and animals. The circus director whom I had chatted with was interviewed, as well as a few of the other circus stars and workers. I couldn't find Marko's picture anywhere. After I'd finished with the paper and drank all my juice I went outside. I wasn't really sure what I was going to do. I was absolutely alone, and would be until Sophia and Alexandra arrived sometime in the late afternoon.

I went out to the horse pasture, and several of the ponies came up to check me out. I made the rounds to see that everything was all right. Then I went over to the paddock where the stallion Bobby Boy, Sunshine, and a small brown mare named Tuva were all hanging out.

Sunshine came up to me, and for a long time I scratched her neck and ran my fingers through her thick mane. She has an outrageously beautiful head with huge dark eyes and a little soft muzzle that just fits in my hand. She nuzzled me in a friendly manner, and I could understand why Angela had bought her. She was a truly enchanting horse, and I hoped that she was pregnant. The father of the foal would be Bobby Boy, Angela's Appaloosa stallion. Angela had imported him from out west, and it was because of him that Angela's ponies came in so many exciting colors.

Bobby is white with black dots spread over his flanks and hindquarters. He also had a good number of black dots on his head. The color pattern is called "leopard spot," and it's not very common.

Bobby usually hangs out in a pasture with the mare that's ready to be bred. Slowly I sauntered over to him and Tuva. Bobby raised his head and observed me carefully with his big, dark eyes before continuing to graze.

I went back into the house and decided to search the bookshelves for an exciting mystery. Granddad has several shelves filled with mysteries, and I soon found one that looked exciting. I placed a lawn chair in the shade under a tree and sat down. A little way away Fandango and Buster stood very close together, swishing their tails to keep each other free from flies. Bumblebees buzzed peacefully, and a warm summer wind whooshed in the treetops. I went inside and poured myself a large glass of cold juice over some ice cubes and became engrossed in an exciting thriller about a real doctor who solved a big murder case on an army base.

At around four o'clock Mom drove into the courtyard. She parked by the house and Sophia and Alexandra jumped out.

"Hi," said Mom happily. "How's it going?"

"Great!" I replied. "Nothing's happened. I'm just sitting here spending a quiet afternoon reading."

Sophia threw a plastic bag in the air and batted it playfully in the air.

"We have soda and chips," she said happily.

"And candies!" added Alexandra. "And we rented a great video. How do you like my new hair color?"

Alexandra had real blonde hair, but now it was jet black. It made her look like Morticia Addams – the Mom on the Addams' family show – but I knew I couldn't say that to her, so I just nodded and smiled.

"Really different color. Quite a change from before!" I said, and quickly went inside the house before I started laughing.

I was already occupying the guest room, so Sophia and Alexandra put their things in Granddad and Angela's room. Sophia and Alexandra seemed to be in good moods and I happily thought that this might be a really fun weekend after all. It had been great to be alone the whole day, but I had to admit that during the last hour I'd been looking forward to some company.

Sophia and Alexandra went out to check on the ponies. Alexandra, who didn't like horses very much, was tickled pink over the sweet miniature Shetland foals. She and Sophia spent a long time in the large pasture enjoying the foals. I read the last chapter in the thriller – which was really suspenseful – and then I started dinner. There were all sorts of greens for a salad, so I cut up them up and made a dressing. In the freezer I found some bread that Granddad had baked, and then I found some cheese and ham in the refrigerator. We sat down and ate and had a great time together. I was really glad that Sophia and Alexandra had come for the weekend.

Later that evening, I decided to go riding for a while, and Sophia and Alexandra biked over to a pond for a short swim.

Fandango gave a big bored yawn when I brought him in from the pasture, and I knew he wasn't the least bit excited about going for a ride. But when the saddle and bridle were in place, he became a little livelier. Since there was no real trail around the farm, I decided to try dressage in a pasture where there weren't any other horses.

My dressage maneuvers weren't successful. The air was still and hot, the flies were crazily biting Fandango, and he spent the whole time throwing his head in irritation and smacking his tail on his hindquarters. Suddenly he stopped dead and stared at a large patch of overgrown shrubbery growing at the edge of the woods, exactly at the spot where the fence divided the pasture we were in from the pasture that the Shetland ponies were playing and grazing. Fandango sniffed agitatedly and I suddenly felt his entire body become tight as a fiddle string.

"What's the matter, little man?" I asked and patted him soothingly on the neck.

I had no idea what he was afraid of. It couldn't be a deer, since Fandango usually isn't scared when he comes across one. And it could hardly be one of the Shetland ponies, since I could see Bobby and the mares grazing a short distance away.

I kicked Fandango and he began to walk against his will, leaning his body away from the bushes. I tried to get him to forget that he was afraid of the bushes, shortening and lengthening the reins to make him stop a few times and pay attention to me.

But nothing helped. Fandango went around in circles with his body bent like a hook. He was tense, and kept glancing sideways at the dangerous bushes that apparently hid some horse-eating monster. He couldn't relax. I finally gave up and carefully trotted, patting him on the neck.

"Okay, boy, you win, we'll ride over and take a look at what's so dangerous," I said and turned him toward the bushes.

Fandango trotted carefully forward and suddenly he stopped and wouldn't go farther. He was just as upset as before. He raised his head and snorted so loud it sounded like a trumpet blast, and I could feel his heart beating against my leg. In amongst the dense bushes I suddenly saw something move ... something red and white ... and blue? I had no idea what it could be, so with squinted eyes I tried to make out what it was.

A second later, a strangely dressed figure jumped out of the bushes – a clown! A real live clown with a made-up face, large checkered pants, enormous shoes and a red wig! He suddenly threw his head back and began to laugh, a wild, hysterical laugh, and at the same time he waved a large white handkerchief. I stared at him without really registering what it was that I was looking at – and Fandango became uncontrollably frightened! He backed up quickly a few steps while snorting with fear, and then he threw himself 180 degrees around and galloped away as fast as his legs could carry him. I lost both stirrups and sat only three quarters upright in the saddle while desperately holding onto his mane in order to keep from flying off.

Fandango went through the open gate and continued into the courtyard, stopping so abruptly at the barn door that there was a long skid mark in the gravel. When he was finally dead still I slid off on the right side. My knees were limp like overcooked spaghetti. It was as if my legs just couldn't support me, and the reins just slid out of my hand before I could stop them. Fandango knew at once that he was loose. He walked away a few steps, snorted with great agitation, and then began to graze on the grass tufts.

A clown? I was totally confused. Did I really see a clown? How could I have seen a clown? I was deep in thought as I slowly walked toward Fandango. A real live clown – in the middle of a horse pasture? Was it real?

With shaking legs I led Fandango into the pasture. There was absolutely nothing there now. The Shetland ponies grazed calmly and nothing was moving in the bushes.

I looked all around. There was no one around that I could see. The bikes were still gone, and I was alone.

Suddenly I got goose bumps. The summer evening wasn't so peaceful anymore. It was scary and threatening. And for the first time in my life, I wished that my little sister and Alexandra were home with me!

Chapter 6

I wasn't going to ride any more this evening. Instead, I unsaddled Fandango and let him graze on the grass by the house while I sat and held him by the halter chain.

Okay, this may sound crazy, but I was absolutely sure I wasn't alone. Fandango offered me some security, but that was the only security I had!

Time after time, I sneaked a look at the large overgrown bushes out there while frightening thoughts swirled around in my head. I tried to calm myself down and think logically, but nothing helped! The creepy thoughts just kept creeping in! The meeting with that clown had been surprising, terrifying, and unreal – all at the same time!

I kept trying to find an ordinary and logical explanation. What if I'd gotten dehydrated and started hallucinating? It was horribly hot, I was riding without a helmet, I was sweaty and shaky … but dehydration usually makes me shiver, and that's all. I'd never heard that anyone could see things from being dehydrated. And besides, I'd read about people in the desert who go around for days without water, but their hallucinations are about oases and water, not clowns jumping out of bushes.

I wondered whether Sophia and Alexandra had decided to play a trick on me? Maybe they came back early and thought it would be cool to scare me. But in that case, where would they have gotten the clown costume? And why didn't they come out laughing themselves silly at how scared I was? No, that didn't make sense …

I knew only one thing for sure. There'd been a clown in the clump of bushes who had jumped out at Fandango and me, laughed his crazy laugh, waved his handkerchief, nearly scared us to death, and then – disappeared. That was exactly what happened!

Just then Sophia and Alexandra biked into the yard. I let Fandango go and hurried toward them with relief.

"What's with you?" Alexandra inquired when she caught sight of my face.

"Your face is as white as a sheet. Have you seen a ghost?" Sophia asked.

I shook my head and took a deep breath.

"You're not going to believe me," I said so softly that it was almost a whisper. "When I was riding, there was a clown in the bushes over by the fence in the pasture. He hopped out of the bushes and scared Fandango, and then he laughed hysterically …"

Sophia and Alexandra looked at each other and then at me.

"What're you talking about?" Sophia said with raised eyebrows. "Have you gone nuts?"

57

"I promise," I said, and nodded toward the bushes. "I'm not kidding. It sounds crazy, but it did happen, and …"

"Hey sis," Sophia said and patted me on my arm. "Calm down. You must have dreamed the whole thing."

"I didn't," I said in exasperation. "You may not believe me, but …"

"Okay, we'll go over and look for some proof," said Alexandra. "If there's a clown there, I'll find him!"

"Of course he'd have left footprints – say, size 19 or so!" giggled Sophia.

"You are so annoying!" I screamed. "Why do you have to go there?"

"To make sure there's nothing dangerous," Alexandra calmly said. "Why don't you go and take Fandango to the barn and we'll go check it out by ourselves."

"But …" I began, and then accepted what she'd said. I had to admit that Sophia and Alexandra's nonchalance had rubbed off on me, and when I talked about the clown he didn't seem so threatening and scary as before.

I led Fandango to the barn and joined them in walking to the bushes. The Shetland ponies were calmly grazing in their pasture. Sunshine raised her beautiful head and took a couple of steps toward us. I turned around and could see something move in the corner of my eye. It looked like a dark shadow that quickly disappeared among the trees.

"There's something over there," I hissed to Sophia. "I saw someone sneak away among the trees! I'm not kidding, it was someone … Sunshine saw it too!"

Sophia and Alexandra looked in the direction that I

pointed, but there was absolutely no movement now. The woods were still and calm, without a single leaf moving in the still summer night.

"What a scaredy cat … you see ghosts everywhere," Sophia sighed as she pushed aside some of the branches in the bush clump.

Among the brush young seedlings had grown, and there was a small green patch of twigs and leaves. The earth was worn down, and I knew the ponies loved to stand there on really warm days to escape the sun and all the flies. Nervously I looked around without really knowing what I was expecting to find. Somewhere deep inside, I was terrified that the clown might still be there – while at the same time, common sense told me that if there was a clown he'd surely taken off a long time ago. On the other hand – if he wasn't still there and hadn't left any trace – how could I expect Sophia and Alexandra to believe that he existed and had really been there?

"Look, there's something on the ground!" I shouted and pointed to a small piece of paper. Alexandra, who was closest to it, bent down and picked it up.

"It's a candy wrapper," she examined it and said. "It's not exactly proof that a crazy clown was here, I'm so sorry to report."

"Well," Sophia said, "I'm beginning to think you've had sunstroke, Sara. You're a nut case! I always knew you were crazy, and this proves it."

"Stop!" I said in a rage. "I'm not crazy!"

"Stop arguing now," Alexandra said. "Let's go inside instead and watch the video we rented!"

"Yeah, I'd forgotten about that! There's nothing here. Let's …" Sophia said. "Hey, wait, what's this?"

Sophia bent down and picked up a notice that had been fastened between the branches. It was a postcard of a clown – a close-up of its face with a large grinning mouth, a red bulbous nose and wild red hair. The clown had a broad smile, but on his cheeks someone had drawn large, blue tears with a felt tip pen.

Sophia turned the card over. On the other side there were three words written in a childish handwriting.

"The clown cries!" Sophia read slowly.

"Oh, no!" said Alexandra, and I could feel her panic.

"Someone must be playing tricks on us," said Sophia as she put the postcard in her pocket. "I couldn't care less. Come on! Let's go inside. I'm as hungry as a wolf!"

I didn't understand how Sophia could blow off the whole postcard thing. I was sure that the clown, the postcard, and the shadow I'd seen disappearing into the woods were all connected! But I didn't say anything more about that … I'd just be laughed at, I thought gloomily, so we went into the house together.

A while later we settled down in the living room. I had crept up in the large armchair and Alexandra and Sophia lay on the sofa. We had chips, soda and goodies to munch on. Alexandra and Sophia ate with gusto, but I was still too unsettled to take more than a cup of watery blackcurrant tea.

We had agreed that the girls would rent a romance, but Alexandra had rented "The Boy in the Grave" at the video store. She'd also found a gruesome thriller in her brother's video collection and brought that along. Naturally, she and Sophia preferred to watch that! I protested because I'd been scared enough for one night, but I was overruled. At first I thought I would just go up to bed instead, but the introduction to the film was so exciting that I wanted to see how it turned out, so I stayed in my chair while the tea cooled and the August night turned pitch black outside the window.

Naturally the hero saved the heroine in the end, but the many grisly scenes didn't help my nerves much.

While Sophia and Alexandra picked up the mess in the living room, I went slowly upstairs. It was dark, so I turned on all the lights. I checked out every nook and cranny to make sure no one was hiding anywhere. Everything was exactly as it should be, and I began to feel a little silly.

Sophia and Alexandra came upstairs, yawning and being a little silly themselves as they settled into Granddad and Angela's huge bed. They talked and laughed for a long time, but instead of me being irritated, I felt myself growing calmer knowing that they were in the room next to mine.

Still, I had a hard time falling asleep, so I lay down in bed and read a bunch of old horse magazines that I found on the bookshelf. Finally, after Alexandra and Sophia quieted down, I turned off the light and tried to fall asleep.

It was peaceful and quiet in the house, and outside the window I could hear a faint wind blowing through the old trees. I shut my eyes and thought about the competition the next week. I thought about Winny, who was still in a pasture in England grazing peacefully, not knowing that she'd soon be moving to the US. I thought about Mike whom I liked so much … and I felt sleepier and sleepier.

Suddenly I was wide-awake, and I strained my eyes in the dark. The door to my room had opened slightly!

I was cold and hot at the same time, and I felt like I couldn't even breathe. Did I really see the door move – or was it my imagination?

But it wasn't my imagination! The door opened carefully, and suddenly it creaked a little.

Help me! I thought, horrified, as I stared at it. I was so scared that I shook and I didn't know what to do – should I shout for help, or just lie still, hoping that I wouldn't be discovered?

Just then I heard the sound of little soft paws on the floor and caught a glimpse of a tiny black shape. It was Angela's cat Mimi!

"Meow?" she requested, and I encouraged her with a "tsk tsk tsk." With a bounding leap, she jumped on the bed and lay down beside me. She purred happily and I lay my arm over her. It felt secure to have her there as I slowly released my fear. I said goodnight to Mimi, and then I felt myself finally slipping off to sleep.

The next time I opened my eyes it was morning and the sun shone through the window curtains. I stretched my legs while still lying in bed. In the morning light yesterday felt like a long, strange dream, and the more I thought about it the more I began to wonder if I had imagined the whole thing after all. At the same time, there was a loud noise on the stairs and I heard Sophia come rushing up, yelling to me. She threw open the door to my room, and I sat up quickly, prepared for the worst.

"Hurry! Get up! Someone broke into the saddle room last night!"

Chapter 7

The saddle room was a total disaster. Someone had put their whole heart and soul into destroying as much as possible.

The Shetland ponies' saddles, reins and halters were in a huge mess on the floor. Someone had put the tack in a pile, poured leather oil all over, and then trampled on it. Some leather halters were lying in a bucket filled with water, and when I lifted up a pair of riding boots they were filled with water. Angela had two small horse pictures that had been hanging on the wall, and they were torn down and the glass was crushed. On top of all that the culprits had sprayed oil all over the windows and walls – everywhere.

I gave a sigh of relief as I realized I'd been careless the night before. I had hung Fandango's saddle over a box stall partition, and then I'd forgotten to put it into the saddle room. It was still hanging there where I left it, along with the bridle, and I was glad that at least *one* thing hadn't been ruined.

"What should we do?" Sophia asked while looking intently at the mess. "Call the police?"

"Yeah, we've got to call them," I nodded. "And also Angela and Granddad."

"I think we should leave everything as it is, until the police have been here," added Alexandra. "But look – what's that?"

She pointed to a paper that was stuck amongst all the bridles. I bent down and carefully took it out. It was a postcard, and I held it between my fingertips by one corner. When I looked carefully at it, my heart started to pound and my mouth was absolutely dry – it was the same postcard we'd found in the bushes the day before! Just like the other postcard someone had drawn blue tears over the smiling clown, and had written on the back the same three words in the same childish handwriting.

"The clown cries!" I read with emphasis.

"How spooky!" Sophia said, sounding scared. "We shouldn't have laughed at you yesterday …"

It was an excellent opportunity for me to get back at Sophia for not believing me yesterday, but I just let it go. Instead I carefully put the postcard back were I found it.

"C'mon – let's go call the police."

It took a long time for the police to arrive, and it was impossible to do anything useful until then. We tried to call Angela, but no one answered. I knew that neither of them liked to be bothered by the cell phone. I could just keep calling, but the cell phone probably lay in their car's glove compartment, either turned off, or with a dead battery.

We checked on the horses frequently, and they thought it was great to have so much attention. Sunshine was so unbelievably cute. Just as I'd done yesterday, I stood and rubbed her soft muzzle.

"*Finally* – they're here," Sophia said, just as the police car turned into the courtyard.

We told the police exactly what had happened, both the night before and today. The police officer, a tall, dark-haired woman, wrote down what we said and asked us a number of questions – such as: Was the tack room locked? *No!* Had this ever happened before? *No!* And so on. We gave her both postcards and told her how we happened to find them. The policewoman said that she would send a crime lab technician who would dust for fingerprints and take some pictures. Until the technician was finished we weren't allowed to go into the tack room, no matter how much we wanted to start cleaning up.

After she left we went to the kitchen to get some food. We weren't particularly hungry, so we didn't eat much. After eating, we found a half-gallon of ice cream in the freezer. A while later, we sat in the sun, enjoying both the ice cream and the sun. For the zillionth time, we replayed what had happened.

Someone was definitely out to frighten us, and they were succeeding. But why would someone want to scare us? None of us had made anybody angry, especially not a clown!

"I'm *sure* this has something to do with Sunshine," Alexandra said after we'd all sat down and made ourselves comfortable in the lawn chairs with our ice cream. "Didn't she come from the circus?"

66

"Yeah," Sophia said. "But it's Angela's horse. Why do this on a weekend when Angela isn't home, if the clown wants to scare her?"

"Besides, Angela bought Sunshine after she went lame and couldn't work as a circus pony any more," I said as I scraped the last bit of ice cream from my dish. "The circus director himself said that he'd called Angela and asked her to buy Sunshine."

"Although that guy ..." I continued, and I suddenly remembered the hateful look the dark-haired man from the circus had given me. "You know, when I rode over here I saw the circus where she came from, and ..."

I told them what had happened, and I hadn't finished telling my story before Alexandra interrupted me.

"The whole thing is perfectly clear! He wants to have Sunshine back at the circus, and he's trying to scare us so Angela won't want to have her here," she burst out, and I nodded.

"Yeah, it can't be a coincidence that a bunch of strange things start to happen exactly when the circus comes to town," Sophia added.

"Uh-huh," Alexandra and I both agreed.

"But what should we do now?" Sophia asked.

"Of course! We'll visit the circus," I said. "It won't take long to bike over there."

"*We'll* bike over and you stay here," Sophia declared. "Alexandra and I borrowed Angela and Granddad's bikes yesterday, and we'll find it easily."

"No way am I staying here alone!" I cried.

"But you *can't* go there because they'll recognize you," Alexandra said.

"Yeah, that's true," I said, hesitantly. "But can't just one of you bike over and one of you stay home with me?"

"Four eyes are better than two," Sophia said quickly. I stuck out my tongue at her. It was so typical of my baby sister to always get her way!

"We won't be long," Alexandra said with assurance. "And now that the police know what happened, you can just call them if you see anything slightly suspicious."

Just then a white car drove into the courtyard. A gray-haired man with a suitcase in his hand jumped out and looked around in a curious way.

"Is this where the break-in took place? Show me the crime scene and the damage," he said in a heavily accented voice.

We told him he had the right place, and then we had to give him our names and social security numbers while he fingerprinted us. It felt a bit strange, but he had to do it so he could tell which fingerprints were different from ours.

Then I took him to the tack room while Sophia and Alexandra got ready to bike over to the circus. I told them to hurry – as long as the police technician was here, I had some company and felt safe, but he wouldn't take all day.

I wanted to watch him while he lifted the fingerprints and collected all the evidence from the tack room, but when I tried to observe from outside the door he rudely waved his hand for me to leave, and told me that he didn't need any help and wanted to be left alone to do his work.

I sighed and went to sunbathe again. Alexandra and Sophia had found a whole stack of magazines in the living room and I browsed through them slowly, not finding anything that caught my interest enough to read.

I went into the kitchen and made some lemonade. Mimi sat on the kitchen bench and licked her front paw very carefully. I petted her a bit before I went out again. I decided to go out and ask the guy from the police department if he wanted some lemonade, but when I got to the courtyard I saw him putting his case back in the car. He looked up at me and took off his latex gloves.

"I'm on my way. I have everything I need," he said. "Somebody will call you with the results on Monday, okay?"

"Would you like some lemonade before you go?" I asked, trying to hide how desperate I was to have company for a little while longer.

"I have to go," he said as he opened the car door. "But thanks anyway! Good bye!"

He started the car with a jarring jump and disappeared from the courtyard in a cloud of dust, and then I was alone.

I looked around. Nothing seemed to have changed in the courtyard, but I still felt that everything was threatening. I looked around and tried to breathe deeply to lessen that unpleasant feeling of fear that sat in my stomach. Slowly I went to the deck chair and sat down again. Mimi came creeping over and hopped up in my arms, and I held her. Just like last night, I felt secure having her purring calmly, and I was glad that at least *she* was home.

From my lookout place I could see most of the horses. Fandango and Buster were grazing peacefully, as were the ponies. Everything looked quiet and safe. But still I knew that it was only an illusion – someone was trying to hurt the horses and us – to hurt us a lot! I got up, still petting Mimi's back. I love to read mystery books where the main character is calm, cool and collected – never scared or nervous. It seems that the nastier things get, the braver she or he becomes … Whereas I am the opposite – tense and anxious the whole time, on high alert, scanning the surroundings and checking out everything around me.

I thought about going inside the house instead of sitting out in the garden, but it felt like it would be scarier to be inside. If I was outside, I could at least run away … I sat and thought about whether I should get Fandango, saddle and bridle him, and have him stand by me just in case I was forced to flee suddenly!

Just then Alexandra and Sophia came peddling into sight.

"Where in the world have you two been?" I shouted to them, as they were still a long way off.

"We haven't been gone that long!" Sophia huffed when she came closer to me. "Only an hour!"

"More like an hour and a half," I said, upset. "Okay, what'd you see at the circus?"

"The circus wasn't there," Sophia said. "They'd already left for their next place, early this morning."

"So, it's probably *not* that strange dark-haired guy who talked about Sunshine when I was there," I said, wondering out loud. "It seemed like he worked at the circus. They were probably busy getting everything packed up to leave, so he probably wouldn't have had time to come here and make that mess."

"True – they packed everything up right after their last performance last night and drove away at the crack of dawn this morning," Alexandra said.

"How'd you find that out?" I wondered.

"We met some guys we knew at the campground," Sophia said nonchalantly. "We stayed and spoke with them for a while, and they told us."

I nodded – and suddenly I knew exactly why their visit to the Circus-That-Wasn't-There took such a long time! I had to sigh – my sister is hopeless!

Chapter 8

"Where in the blazes are they?" I said nervously as I slammed the receiver down. "I've called home, and I've also tried both Mom and Dad's cell phones. No one answers!"

"No idea," Sophia replied calmly.

I gave a deep sigh and sunk down in a kitchen chair.

"Typical! What should we do now?"

"Try to call Granddad and Angela again," Sophia said. "Get them to come home immediately. It's quite simple."

"Easy for you to say," I moaned. "They're two counties away at the pony show, or did you forget? It's a few hundred miles to get there and back!"

"How 'bout *your* parents?" Sophia asked Alexandra.

"My dad's away at a conference and Mom works nights," Alexandra said, twirling a pencil between her fingers. "It's no use calling them," she added.

"Okay, so what do we do now?" Sophia asked.

"No idea," I said.

"We can stand watch tonight," Sophia said. "We'll take

turns sleeping. If something happens, then the one on watch will wake the others."

I nodded. "That sounds like a great idea. If we all sleep we could be taken by surprise if someone comes to make trouble – and that's not a comforting thought!"

"Should we go out and straighten up the tack room a little?" Alexandra suggested. "It's still light out. There's a good movie on at ten that I want to watch."

"The heck with cleaning," Sophia said and stuck out her tongue.

"Cut it out," I said to Sophia sternly. "Do you think it's fair to leave all the cleaning for Angela and Granddad when they come home on Monday?"

"No, not really," Sophia grumped, following along against her will.

We realized that we'd never be able to clean up the whole mess in one night, but we could at least get started salvaging whatever *could* be saved. Sophia emptied water from the riding boots and everything else that was full of water. Then she began to hang up the saddle pads one at a time on the stall walls to see how damaged they were. Fortunately only the pads that were on the top of the pile had gotten saturated with oil and dirt. The others only had a few spots of oil on them.

Alexandra hung up the halters to dry, and then we did our best to sort out the pile of saddles and bridles on the floor. It wasn't really as difficult as it looked at first, because the person who did it seemed to have tossed everything in one big pile and left it while he moved on to destroy other stuff.

Finally all the gear was hung up, and Sophia looked around.

"Everything that was sprayed with oil we will clean tomorrow," she said, and we both nodded.

"It would probably be best to take everything out of the tack room and hit it with a high pressure water hose," I suggested. "But Granddad can do that when he comes home on Monday."

"Exactly," said Sophia as she pushed the hair away from her forehead and eyes. Her hands were filthy, and left a long dark stripe across her forehead.

"Wow, this leather oil stinks worse than a skunk!" she said sniffing her hands.

"Do you really think so?" Alexandra asked. "I like the smell."

"Hmmm, it's probably because my Dad used to make us scrub all the leather things clean and then oil them when we were little. It took hours, and our hands and nails were totally destroyed for days," Sophia said gloomily as she examined her filthy hands.

"You have to oil leather things every now and then or they won't keep," I said.

"I surrender! Dad really succeeded in brainwashing you," Sophia sighed, raising her eyebrows in disbelief.

"Come on, guys," Alexandra said, breaking us up before an argument could really get going. "The show's about to start!"

"Okay," Sophia agreed. "There's popcorn in the pantry."

"Yum, yum," I said as we turned off the lights, shut the door, and half-ran to the house.

It was very dark; we could see the stars blinking in the clear sky. Usually I thought these warm, dark August nights were beautiful. It was a nice cozy feeling that I got at the end of summer. But now the darkness felt like a threat. I knew that someone could be hiding out there right now, just waiting. The whole yard was full of dark shadows, and an owl suddenly let out a hoot. I froze with fear, but then calmed down and kept on going toward the house.

It felt so good to get inside and turn on all the lights. We went around and checked to make sure all the windows were shut, and then we locked the door carefully with both locks. I was sure that Sophia and Alexandra thought that I was silly to do that, but neither of them said anything, so I guess they were a little scared too – even if they were pretending not to be.

We made some more lemonade and microwaved some cinnamon buns from the freezer. We popped the popcorn, and spread out our snacks on the sofa table in front of the TV. The movie was a really good one. Mimi came in quietly and plopped down on my lap, purring loudly.

"That cat ought to have a muffler," Sophia said with a yawn. "Boy, I'm unbelievably tired."

"You should try to sleep." Alexandra said, throwing her a pillow. "I don't think I can stay awake either!"

"Me neither," I said as an afterthought. I peeked out into the dark from the large living room window.

It felt safe with all three of us together, but I couldn't stop an unpleasant feeling that drained my courage. It was a dark

August night, and just outside were the woods, totally black and threatening …

"Yikes, doesn't it feel scary?" Alexandra said as if she were reading my mind. "If somebody is out there in the dark, he can see right into the living room."

"I was just thinking the same thing," I said with a quivering voice as I pulled my blanket tighter around me. Mimi looked annoyed at me for making her move over before she could lie down and get comfortable again.

"I wish there were blinds or shades that we could pull down," Alexandra said, and I nodded.

"Do you want to go upstairs instead?" she suggested, but Sophia shook her head.

"There's no TV up there," she said as she crammed a whole fistful of popcorn into her mouth. "Stop being such a scaredy cat. You're so easy to scare."

"Easy for you to say," I said sulkily. "I've seen the clown once up close, and experienced his nasty surprises twice …"

"Three times, if you count the tack room," Alexandra interrupted.

"Yeah, I forgot, but you're just spooking yourself now!" Sophia said yawning. "And besides, I don't believe that –"

A short knock at the window made her stop in the middle of the sentence, and we all three stared at the window where the clown pressed his made-up face against the glass.

He must have had a flashlight in his hand, because his face was lit from under his chin. The light made him look twisted and threatening. I felt my blood freeze in my veins. Alexandra let out a horrendous scream and covered her head with the blanket. Mimi was terrified, and she sprang out of my arms and rushed into the kitchen. I was paralyzed and just stared at the clown who carefully took out a large white handkerchief and wiped a tear from his cheek.

"The clown's crying …" Sophia mumbled, and suddenly she sprang up, just as fast, but not as gracefully as Mimi.

"Now I'm going to find out who that guy is!" she roared, and before I could stop her, she rushed to the front door.

"Sophia! STOP!" I screamed, and ran after her. I tripped on the blanket I had over my legs, and before I could free myself from the blanket I heard the door open and Sophia running down the steps.

"You cowardly idiot!" she screamed at the top of her lungs. She waved Granddad's huge flashlight and let the strong beam fly to the right and the left around the garden.

"You puny, despicable rat! Come out and tell us who you are, instead of acting like a stupid clown."

"Stop being a jerk!" I said from behind her. "Stop it and come inside!"

"COME OUT NOW!" Sophia hollered, but nothing moved in the garden, and I knew that the person who scared us was already far away.

Sophia came in and slammed the door with a huge bang as I quickly locked it.

"You're completely nuts!" I shouted at her. "What in the blazes were you doing? Don't you realize that he could be dangerous?"

77

"Dangerous?" Sophia sniffed "I doubt it. It's just someone who wants to scare us. If he were really dangerous he would have tried something much worse already."

"How can you know that?" Alexandra asked as she reappeared in the living room, her face ghost-white, and her eyes filled with tears. "You could have been murdered. That clown person isn't in his right mind. I want to go home!"

Sophia looked like an angry bull.

"I don't understand why you're so afraid," she said angrily as she put down the flashlight. "Attack's always the best defense."

"Really?" I said with raised eyebrows. "You know that for a fact?"

"Yes, well," Sophia said as she went into the living room and turned off the TV. "If any of us are afraid, it's that guy. He's the coward."

"You've totally snapped," I said. "SNAPPED! Do you hear me? You're crazy!"

At the same time, I couldn't help but admire Sophia. It was really dumb what she did, but all the same, she'd really scared off the clown. He'd disappeared with unbelievable speed!

"And now I'm going to call the police," I said as I grabbed the phone receiver and dialed the number from memory. I heard a totally strange signal, and then the operator forwarded me from the large police station in town to the night duty person at a smaller site. This person sounded like a grumpy old man who listened with indifference as I told him the story. After he had written it up, along with my name and address, he said if something further happened we should call him.

"Can't you come here or send someone out, please?" I asked, but he just sighed and said there was no way that was happening. And besides, he was sure it was just one of our boyfriends playing a prank on us!

You'd better believe I was angry when I hung up! But it didn't matter. We wouldn't get any help from him no matter what. We simply had to figure out what we needed to do to protect ourselves!

"Okay," Sophia yawned. "Which one of us wants to stand watch first?"

"I don't think I can go to sleep," Alexandra said with a definite tone and took her blanket and pillow. "I think I'll go upstairs and sit in the easy chair there. And I'll stay there for the whole night."

"It's a good idea for all of us to go upstairs," I said to Sophia. "Then we can turn out all the lights and just sit and watch to see if he comes back."

Sophia nodded.

"Okay. I think I'll go around and check one more time to see if the windows are shut tight and that the outer doors are double locked," she said.

"Do you want me to come too?" I asked, and Sophia nodded.

"Sure, c'mon."

"I don't want to be alone," Alexandra said, and she put her blanket down. "I'm coming too!"

We went around the whole downstairs and tested all the windows, the front door and the cellar door. We felt better when we finally went upstairs; we weren't as afraid any more. Even Alexandra and I had caught some of Sophia's rage and courage. Mimi came out again and pattered up the stairs after us. It seemed as if she understood that Alexandra was the most scared, because she jumped on her lap and started to purr as soon as Alexandra had spread out her blanket and settled down in Granddad's reading chair.

Granddad's chair is a recliner, and Alexandra let the back down and pushed out the footrest so she was half-lying down. I lay down on my bed fully clothed, and every now and then I went to the windows and looked out.

We had turned off all the lights in the whole house, and as soon as our eyes adjusted to the darkness we could pick out a lot of details.

The only light source was the outer lamp mounted on the barn wall, but it was too weak to light up all the shadows and dark corners. It would be easy for someone to hide, I thought to myself.

I wondered if I ought to check on the horses? I wasn't the least worried about Fandango and Buster. They usually went into the woods in the night to escape the mosquitoes, but I worried about whether the clown would leave the Shetland ponies alone.

What if he didn't? Maybe I should go down and bring them in? I didn't know what to do … I couldn't lock the barn, so maybe they were more protected out in the dark? Sophia had lain down on Granddad and Angela's bed.

Every now and then she went over to the windows on her side of the house and, as if on a schedule, we would sneak over and make sure Alexandra was still awake. She'd finally fallen asleep in the chair, sleeping so deeply that neither of us wanted to wake her. It would be better if she stood watch in the morning after dawn, when it wouldn't be so creepy.

The hours went by and nothing more happened. In a little while the sky began to lighten and turn pink as the new day swept over the landscape. A thin white film of fog lay over the fields and pastures, and when the sun's first rays hit, dew glittered in the garden. I yawned a huge yawn and pulled my blanket tighter around me. I was glad the night was over. Today was Sunday and tomorrow Granddad and Angela would be home again. And maybe then we would find out what the clown wanted.

Chapter 9

During the early morning hours Sophia and I slept while Alexandra stayed awake and watched over the house and yard. The sun continued to shine from a clear blue sky, and it was another wonderful late summer day. At about ten o'clock I tried to call Mom on her cell phone, and she finally answered. She sounded incredibly tired as she picked up the phone with a yawn.

"Where are you?" I asked.

"In the city." Mom said. "What's up?"

"What'd you mean – the city?" I burst out. "What in the world are you doing there?"

"We dined, danced, and … well …" Mom said, sounding almost as guilty as Sophia does when she's been out partying.

"But …" I said, although I knew at that same time there was no way she'd be able to help us.

"What do you want?" Mom continued. "Are you having fun? Is everything okay?"

"Yeah, we are," I said. "The sun's shining and it's a beautiful day."

Sophia, who sat on one of the kitchen chairs, made an angry face at me, and I knew she was mad that I making small talk and avoiding the truth.

After a little more chitchat, I hung up, and barely took a breath before Sophia demanded to know why in blazes I hadn't told Mom what was happening.

"They're in the city," I sighed. "They won't be home until sometime tonight."

"What're they doing there?" Alexandra asked.

"Having fun," I said. Mom has buddies that they stay with sometimes.

"But why didn't you tell them what happened?" Sophia said obstinately, and I shrugged my shoulders.

"Why? They'd be worried and they'd come rushing home immediately. We can get help somewhere else," I said.

Feeling discouraged, we sat at the kitchen table a bit longer, not saying anything. Finally Sophia took out her phone and announced that she was going to call the police. But their line was busy, and after a few minutes stuck on hold she hung up.

I tried to call Angela's cell phone one more time, but they still didn't answer. Then Alexandra called her mom, but she was probably still asleep after her work night, and had the ringer turned down or off.

"This is unbelievable," hissed Sophia angrily as she poured herself some juice. "When I want to be left alone – then the adults are all over me, butting into everything I do. But when I *really* need them, they're gone with the wind!"

Alexandra and I nodded. There was a lot of truth in what she said …

We went out for a tour around the place to see if the clown had left anything in the barn or paddocks during the night, but we couldn't find anything.

The horses grazed on the green grass, the foals played, and Bobby calmly hung out with both his mares. Sunshine came up to me and gave me a friendly greeting and I caressed her neck and mane.

"Do you know what?" Alexandra said, and I shook my head.

"I think the strangest thing about all of this is that the clown doesn't seem to have any reason for what he's doing," she said. "I mean – he hasn't stolen anything, nothing is missing, he hasn't tried to break into the house, and the horses are still here and just as they should be."

"He is, well – crazy in some way," Sophia said. "I think he's just out to scare us!"

"But why *us*?" Alexandra asked. "There's no reason!"

"I've been thinking about the motive too," I said "and I think it's somehow tied to Sunshine and that guy from the circus."

"I agree," Sophia said. "That's the only thing I can think of."

"Like I said before – maybe he didn't like it that the circus director sold Sunshine, and now he wants to scare us so Angela will give her back," Alexandra said while we slowly walked back to the house.

"But Angela bought her because she couldn't perform in

the circus show any more," I said. "That's what makes this so strange!"

"Maybe he doesn't care about that," Alexandra said. "Maybe he loves Sunshine more than anything, and … maybe he wants revenge of some sort."

"Hey, did we really leave the door open like that?" Sophia said suspiciously and pointed toward the veranda. "I'm sure I shut and locked it …"

All three of us stood on the gravel and looked at the door.

"It could've opened by itself," I said nervously. "The latch is old and worn out."

"I doubt it," Sophia said. "There's something funny going on here."

"Do you think he's in the house?" Alexandra whispered, and I heard the fear in her voice. She grabbed Sophia's arm and her raw nerves gave my stomach a hard knot of uncertainty.

"How do I know?" Sophia said and I finally heard a little fear in her voice.

"Should we go in and look?" I asked, and I felt my stomach cramp up in dread. "Or do either of you have your cell phone with you so we can call the police?"

"My cell phone's in there," Alexandra said anxiously. "You have yours, I hope?"

Both Sophia and I shook our heads no.

"At least it's three against one," Sophia said, pretending to be her usual cocky self. "Let's go in now!"

"Are you crazy?" Alexandra said. "We don't dare!"

"Will you be okay staying here alone?" I asked as we looked around us. The sun was shining, the bees were buzzing and the horses grazed peacefully in their pastures. It was a normal wonderful late summer day – and yet it felt like something horrible might happen at any moment.

"What do you want to do? Wait until someone comes and rescues us?" Sophia said. "C'mon. We have to go inside."

"But …" Alexandra said doubtfully, but she didn't say another word, and with Sophia in the lead we went toward the house.

"What if he's looking out one of the windows and sees us?" Alexandra whispered in fear as we approached the veranda. "I don't think I dare …"

"Be quiet," I hissed. "You're making us more scared."

We were really jittery when we entered the house. My heart was pounding so hard that I was sure everyone could hear it, and my mouth was completely dry. We stayed close together and tried to look in all directions at the same time. We were making certain that the clown couldn't take us by surprise. The house revealed nothing out of the ordinary. We soon got a little braver, and as several more minutes passed, it seemed unlikely that he was inside. Nothing had been touched or moved, the safe in Angela's office was still locked, and the cups that we had used for our juice were still on the kitchen table in their same places.

We searched the whole house as a team. We opened the closet doors, looked under the sofa and beds and even in the coat closet in the hall. We looked everywhere except down in the cellar. That we ignored. None of us had any desire to go down there, and besides, the cellar door was still locked. The only key to that door was hanging on a nail in its usual place in the kitchen. No one could hide in the cellar and lock the door without taking the key, so we felt relieved.

We were standing together in the hall and I was just about to say that we'd imagined the whole thing when I heard a soft thud in the living room.

"Did you hear that?" Alexandra whispered, and she seemed to be near tears. "He's in there! I want to go home …"

"Calm yourself," Sophia said, and we froze to the spot. "Be quiet …"

I hardly dared to breathe while we stood dead still, scanning the area with our eyes and listening for more sounds.

A second later Mimi came slinking out into the hall . She meowed loudly and began to weave and rub in and out through my legs.

"Of course, it was that darned cat!" Sophia said with relief.

"Are you sure?" Alexandra said in a voice full of doubt.

"I'm absolutely sure," I said as I gathered Mimi in my arms. "That was a typical Mimi thud!"

I felt like giggling now that everything dangerous had passed. Sophia had simply forgotten to close the door, and that was all there was to it. We'd all imagined the worst and gotten ourselves scared out of our wits. If we hadn't already been so worked up, we certainly would never have thought anything about the open door.

We went into the kitchen and Sophia began to search the refrigerator for something to eat. I sat down at the kitchen table and Alexandra dared to tiptoe though the hallway to the bathroom.

We were absolutely giddy after all the excitement, and Mimi thought we were noisy jokers. She sat straight up in one of the kitchen chairs licking one of her front paws carefully, and seemed to be in deep thought about cat affairs.

I was just putting the plates down on the table when I noticed something strange. Under the little red placemat on the kitchen table was a corner of a piece of paper sticking out. I pulled it with my hand and the front side of a postcard became visible.

"Sophia!" I cried out in a horrified voice.

It was just like the other two postcards! There was a clown, and on the clown's cheeks someone had painted large blue tears with a magic marker. On the backside in the same horribly childish handwriting as the other two someone had written, *The clown cries …*

"So he *was* in here!" I said, and felt as if I couldn't breathe.

Sophia nodded, and I saw that the color had drained from her face. Alexandra, who had just come back into the kitchen, stared in horror at the postcard, her mouth hanging open and her eyes filled with tears.

"I can't stay here any longer," she whimpered and sniffled.

"Right," I said and grabbed my cell phone. "This is enough! Now that grumpy old man at the police station *has* to get someone out here to help us!"

Once again I dialed the police, and this time a different person answered. He sounded friendly and understanding. He said we absolutely had to make a complaint, about what happened last night and about the clown being in the house today.

"Can you come down to the police station and do it?" he asked, and I just sighed.

"No, none of us has a car," I said. "Can't you come here? Maybe there are clues or prints that can reveal his identity."

The policeman was silent for a bit, and then he said that he would try to send a car, but it couldn't be right away, so we might have to wait a while. I made a silent grimace at Sophia and Alexandra who sat anxiously listening to my side of the phone conversation.

When I was finished with the policeman, Alexandra called her mom. She had just woken up after having slept almost the whole morning, and when Alexandra told her everything that had happened, she became wide awake and worried.

"I'll be right over, as quickly as I can dress and drive there," she said to Alexandra. "Just stay there and don't go outside!"

Alexandra nodded and hung up the phone.

"Mom's coming here," she said smiling. "Finally!"

"Yeah," I said. "That's a relief!"

Just then I glanced out the kitchen window – and jerked my head around and stared. Was I dreaming, or …? No, this was real!

"Sophia – Alexandra!" I shrieked. "Look out there!"

Outside of the house, Bobby, Sunshine and the other little

89

mare were trotting by. The clown was running behind them, dressed in his oversized clown clothes and a pair of enormous shoes. He shooed the ponies with his large handkerchief, and they ran willingly in front of him.

Then they trotted out of the courtyard, and disappeared behind the lilac bushes. I stared at Alexandra and Sophia.

"We have to stop him!" Sophia shouted. "He's totally insane!"

"I'll get Fandango," I said, jumping up from the chair so fast that it went over backwards. "It's our only chance!"

I rushed out to Fandango and Buster who both stood at the gate with erect ears. They had certainly seen the clown shoo Bobby and his girlfriends away, and were probably wondering what was going on.

Fandango and Buster's halters were lying just outside the pasture gate. With shaking hands I grabbed Fandango's halter, fastened it to some reins, secured it around his head, and quickly led him through the gate. I managed to climb on his back, and Fandango and I started after them at a full gallop through the garden and down the gravel road. With this speed I was sure to catch up to them soon – although I wasn't really sure what I was going to do when I did. Whatever happens, happens, I thought, both furious and scared at the same time.

But as I got near where they should have been, it was the strangest thing. It seemed like the clown and the ponies had been swallowed up by the earth – I couldn't see them anywhere. At first I didn't have a clue as to where they went! They had to be around here somewhere, right? They couldn't have gotten too far in such a short amount of time. The clown hadn't looked able to move very fast when I'd seen him shooing the ponies in his humongous shoes.

Suddenly a thought came to me – maybe they'd taken the *other* way to the main highway – the one that Fandango and I had taken when we'd ridden here the other day.

After about a hundred yards I succeeded in reining in Fandango so I could turn him and go in the other direction. I sat glued to the saddle when he began to gallop toward home with long strides. The wind on my hair and face made me realize how fast we were going, and that I didn't have my helmet on. I sneaked a glance at the gravel road that flew by under Fandango's thundering hooves and realized for an ice-cold sobering nanosecond that if I fell off at this speed I would die …

Fear made me grab his mane, and I was thankful that I'd ridden so much bareback over the years.

I saw the small road up ahead to the right. It felt like half an eternity since I'd come riding along this road on my way to Granddad and Angela's. I tried to rein in Fandango, and strangely enough he actually seemed to listen to me although he still kept going fast. Maybe he was beginning to get tired, or maybe he knew I was serious?

"Calm down, boy … slow down …" I mumbled as Fandango threw his head in irritation. He didn't want to slow down now when it was so much fun to gallop, and besides, he was heading home! I kept on talking to him calmly, and just a few yards before we reached the road that went off to the right he finally slowed down to a bumpy, uncomfortable, jerking trot. I pulled hard on the right rein and kicked him the hardest I could with my left leg and, incredibly, he obeyed and headed down the path through the woods without any big fuss.

I reined him in to a slow walk and began to examine the ground, hoping to find some tracks. As luck would have it before Fandango began to trot again I found the impressions of small hooves in the soft sand.

"Darn it! Why didn't I take this way first?" I mumbled extremely unhappily and pushed Fandango forward. He answered willingly, and soon we thundered along the path at the finest race speed ever. I stopped thinking about how dangerous this could be – I was determined to catch up to the clown and ponies before they reached the highway!

Fandango was quick, and it didn't take long before the gate appeared in front of us.

Fandango remembered that he had jumped it before. He raised his head as he raced toward it, just like it was a cavaletti.

I saw the gate coming closer and closer, and had no chance to stop Fandango. Unhappily I grabbed his mane again and squeezed with my legs as hard as I could. The gate, which had seemed like a small obstacle two days ago, now stretched before us like a giant barrier. It had grown taller by a few feet. I grasped his mane tighter, tried to squeeze harder with my legs, and then I felt Fandango once again lift himself over the gate with a good margin.

When he landed I slid forward, almost falling off – but oddly enough it seemed like Fandango maneuvered to keep me sitting on him. He took a pair of bizarre, angled gallop strides that put me back in the saddle, and I promptly patted him on the neck. He really is a fantastic horse – my beloved pony!

We continued toward the highway at a little calmer gallop, and I kept scanning the whole time for the ponies. When we came to the highway I succeeded in slowing Fandango down, and he danced around excitedly on the asphalt. Luck was with us as there were no cars and I was able to rein him in while I looked around quickly.

Suddenly I caught sight of the three Shetland ponies and the clown! A long way from us, right before the entrance to the highway, the clown was running along the edge of the large field. He no longer had his big shoes – it looked like he had regular gym shoes, or something like that.

Bobby trotted beside him, and the clown held him by the halter while the two mares ran loose.

I saw the clown stop and look around. Then he continued toward the highway with the three ponies. When he was almost to the fence that keeps wild animals from crossing, he let go of Bobby's halter and once again shooed the ponies with his large white handkerchief.

I could hear the traffic on the highway overpass speeding by, and I began to sob. The cars would never have a chance to stop if the three ponies ran out in front of them … not only could the ponies die, but so could a lot of innocent people!

"We have to stop him!" I screamed and dug my heels into Fandango's sides. "C'mon! Faster!"

Chapter 10

"We *must* make it, we *must* get there in time," drummed through my head in time with Fandango's galloping gait. Just ahead I saw the clown herd the small ponies toward the opening in the wild animal protection fence. The fence was just at the off ramp from the highway, and it was also the only place where it was possible to go *up* to the highway.

In front of the ponies, just on the other side of the protective fence, I could see the broad highway with its four lanes and heavy traffic. The noise from the huge trucks on the overpass, where Fandango and I had gone under just a few days ago, was alarmingly close. And with each step the ponies took, the danger increased!

When they reached the opening in the fence the clown shooed the ponies so they would move faster. He screamed at them and waved his large handkerchief wildly, and the ponies reacted by trotting faster. They were on their way up the gravel slope to the edge of the asphalt when Bobby stopped dead in his tracks. He raised his head and looked at the cars suspiciously as they sped by at 65 miles an hour.

The two mares followed his example. The clown took hold of Bobby's halter and tried to pull him forward up onto the asphalt, but the little stallion refused to move. He snorted a warning, and at that moment a huge tractor-trailer truck on the highway tooted his horn – a deafening racket that echoed in the air.

Maybe the driver saw and sensed what was about to happen? I hoped so!

"Go on, go on!" I heard the clown scream, and in the next second he hit Bobby on his neck with his handkerchief! But Bobby threw himself to the side, making the clown lose his grip on Bobby's halter. And instead of running onto the highway, Bobby turned 90 degrees to the left, and with the mares following him he galloped away on the right side of the fence.

I screamed, "Yes, that's the way!" and turned Fandango toward the three small galloping ponies.

On the other side of the tall protection fence, people in their cars glared at the three fleeing ponies with Fandango and me in full gallop after them. I didn't give a hoot what they thought! The ponies were safe from danger now, and whatever the clown had planned, he couldn't stop them. Besides, I had driven along the highway thousands of times, and I knew that the protective fence ran for miles all the way into town without any more openings or on-ramps.

Bobby slowed down to a trot, and then to a walk, and Fandango and I rode up beside him. The ponies stopped without really knowing where they should go next, and Bobby looked angrily at Fandango with his ears flat back.

He threw back his beautiful head, screamed a challenge, and stamped the ground with one of his front hooves. He obviously saw Fandango as a rival for his mares, so I rode a short distance away and we stayed there. The ponies were still upset after their forced march; they were breathing heavily and Bobby trotted around the mares a couple of times. Sunshine leaped to the side when a huge trailer truck thundered by, and little Tuva looked like she was prepared to gallop away again. I tried to talk calmly to them from where I sat on Fandango, but they didn't seem to tune in to anything I said.

Finally Sunshine sucked in a deep breath, and then bent her head down and started to graze on the short, sweet grass – and soon the other two followed her lead.

Now that the ponies had finally calmed down, I turned Fandango around and looked for the clown, but he was gone! Furiously, I muttered a whole string of angry words to myself. Once again, he'd gotten away!

Just then I heard the police sirens coming closer, and two police cars came along the highway with their blue lights flashing.

I waved to them and one car stopped at the roadside. A pair of young policemen in uniform hopped out. The other car continued on to the highway exit ramp where they swung off and parked by the side of the ditch next to the large open field where the ponies and I were.

"Is everything all right, Sara?" the policeman asked as he came toward us, and I realized that I recognized him. It was Andrew Roos, and he had the same short-cut blond hair and little thin mustache. He had helped Mike and me earlier this summer when we succeeded in saving a bunch of stolen horses that were going to be sold for slaughter.

"Yeah, everything's fine now, Officer Roos," I said, and suddenly my whole body shook with a sense of well-being.

"There aren't any horses on that side of the fence are there?" his colleague, a young dark-skinned guy, asked, and I shook my head.

"That's good!" Andrew said. "Can you manage to get the horses home, or do you need help?"

"I need help," I said. "I don't have any ropes or anything …"

"A tow line will do," Andrew said, and he and his colleague jumped in the car and drove over to the other car.

A few minutes later Andrew came running back with three towropes. With skillful hands, he fastened them to Bobby and the mares' halters, and then we went at a leisurely pace, leading the ponies back to the cars.

"Wow, what little horses," a young blonde policewoman said as she looked wide-eyed at the ponies.

"They're mini Shetland ponies," I said.

"They're not any bigger than our police dogs," said the woman, shaking her head in disbelief.

"How far is it to the farm where these three tiny things live?" Andrew asked.

"A couple of miles at the most," I said. "It's on the other side of the woods."

The police discussed the situation for a few moments, and then Andrew came over and said he would lead the three ponies to Granddad's. I stayed mounted on Fandango in spite of the extreme discomfort. He was wet with sweat, and I was covered with his hair strands on the inside of my legs. I was hot, sweaty and itched like I had poison ivy. I decided that after we jumped the gate I would definitely get down and walk the rest of the way home.

One police car went back to the station while the other drove in front of us to the farm. Andrew and I turned into the woods with the horses, and when the gate appeared in front of us I shortened the reins.

"Please move over to the side, because we need to jump the gate. It's locked, and Fandango's too big to creep under it like the three little ones."

"Did you jump over the gate on the way out?" Andrew asked me with raised eyebrows, and I nodded yes and turned red from embarrassment.

"Without a helmet or saddle on the horse or anything?" he asked and looked sternly at me. I nodded.

"I had no choice," I mumbled. "I wouldn't have been able to catch them otherwise. And I don't have a key!"

"Okay," Andrew said, "but I've got one! And I will *not* allow you to jump over that gate when you're with me. It's not safe and, strictly speaking, you shouldn't even be sitting on that horse!"

He strode forward, unlocked the gate, and held it open for us. I slid off Fandango's back and felt my legs shake. It was as if all my strength had run out. I felt sick and dizzy, and I leaned into Fandango's side as he stood so nicely still.

"Are you feeling okay?" Andrew asked as he shut the gate behind us. "Your face is really white. Are you alright?"

"No, I feel sick," I panted and turned away from Fandango because I felt I might lose the entire contents of my stomach.

"It's okay, it's the shock, and it'll go away," Andrew comforted me as I took several deep-calming breaths.

"Just take is easy," he added. "It's really common to get this kind of reaction after a while. It's not dangerous, but it sure feels unpleasant."

"I thought all the horses were going to run up onto the highway," I cried while trying to stifle my sobs. My eyes were filled with tears and I leaned into Fandango and sobbed. I fully realized how scary this had been and how horribly it could have ended, and I couldn't shake the thought!

"I know you were scared," Andrew said kindly. "Do you want to rest a while before we go on?"

I tried to calm myself down by breathing deeply, and then I shook my head no. I wanted to go home and I wanted everything to be normal again! I wished my Granddad and Angela would come home, the clown would disappear, and Mom and Dad would come home from the city and help us sort out all the horrible things that had happened. Leading Fandango, I slowly walked toward the farm. Andrew went behind us with the three Shetland ponies like dogs on a leash and Fandango, who suddenly realized that I was beginning to pull myself together, tried the whole time to take advantage by biting off leaves from the bushes as we passed.

It felt like it took forever to get home again. A police car stood in the courtyard and Sophia, Alexandra and Andrew's colleague sat in the lawn chairs drinking juice.

They looked so calm and relaxed that I knew, at once, everything was going to be better!

Sophia came hurrying forward and took care of Fandango while Alexandra showed Andrew where the other three ponies lived. I sank down in a garden chair and the other policeman shook my hand and introduced himself as Sandy Carson. Exhausted, I feebly filled a glass to the rim with cold juice and downed it with thirsty gulps.

Sophia and Alexandra had already been told what had happened; but now I had to tell my version while Sandy took notes and Andrew asked questions.

While we sat there in the afternoon sun, everything felt just like a nightmare: the clown, all the anxiety, the weird postcards, and the frantic ride to the highway. But it wasn't a dream – it was plain, harsh reality!

"I can't believe we're going to find the reason behind all of this," I said at last. "Who in this world would be after us three? I haven't crossed anyone. And it's not likely it's Angela that he's after – she's not even home!"

"Hmmm, I can't say why," Andrew said thoughtfully. "To me, it sounds like a mentally ill person who feels he has a reason to hold a grudge. I don't think you should stay here alone tonight."

I nodded. It felt nice to have him say that, and Sophia and Alexandra nodded too.

"My mom's on her way here," Alexandra said. "I wouldn't dare have us stay here by ourselves any longer!"

"The next time we could be his targets!" Sophia said.

"Precisely," Andrew said. "But you have no idea at all why someone would want to hurt either this farm, you, or your Granddad and Angela?"

"The only thing I can think of is that maybe it has something to do with the circus. Sunshine originally belonged to the circus that was at the campgrounds the day before yesterday. There was a guy who worked there as a clown who was very attached to her, and he was angry that she'd been sold."

"That sounds like something we need to check out," Sandy said and made a note. "Do you know where the circus is now?"

"It's not far from here," Andrew said. "They just moved to the other side of town. It's a good circus, and usually comes here once a year."

"We thought it had already moved to another town, so that it would be too difficult for someone from the circus to get here," I said.

"But if it's only a few miles away, then it's a simple matter to bike over or drive a car here, change into a clown suit and make a nuisance of yourself," Sandy said seriously. "We'll swing by the circus on the way home and question them."

"I'm going to call home while you're still here," said Alexandra, and she got up to call.

"Yes, go and do it now, because we have to go soon," said Andrew, and Alexandra nodded as she ran into the house.

When Alexandra finally came back she was grinning happily, and I knew that she'd talked with her mom.

"Mom was on her way out to the car," she said gladly. "Oh, I am so relieved! She'll be here in ten minutes."

"Great," Andrew said.

The two policemen stayed until Alexandra's mom arrived, and then we had to explain everything that had happened all over again. Alexandra's mom was very upset, and she made us call Mom and Dad and ask them to drive here directly when they came back from the city. A while later the two policemen got up and went to their car. I followed them, since I still had to go to the pasture and check on Fandango to make sure he was okay after our wild gallop.

As the police were driving away, Andrew rolled down his window and turned toward me.

"You will of course call us *immediately* if anything suspicious happens, no matter how unimportant it seems," he said. "There's not much action in town for us now, so with a little luck we could get out here right away." He smiled, waved and drove carefully out of the courtyard.

I stared at the disappearing police car and felt goose bumps, even though I knew his words were meant to make me feel secure. But what he said had me anxious, and reminded me that we were still at risk.

Chapter 11

We showed Alexandra's mom, Gail, around the farm, pointing out where we found the different postcards, where the clown had appeared, and everything that he did. She became increasingly upset. Moreover she scolded me, because I hadn't told my mom when she and I were on the phone earlier.

"You understand that they'd want to know right away if something terrible was happening to you," she said and went to call them on her cell phone.

It so happened that our parents were already on their way home, as Dad apparently didn't feel well. And a little over an hour later they pulled into Granddad and Angela's driveway. They had come directly from the city where they apparently had too much fun the night before. Mom still had her eye shadow and mascara on and was wearing high heel shoes with blue jeans! Dad looked exhausted, was red-eyed, his hair stood on end, and he complained about feeling ill. Do I need to add that Mom had driven home?

"How much fun did you actually have?" Gail asked when we sat out on the lawn chairs.

"Too much," sighed Dad. "And besides, I'm sick to my stomach – indigestion from bad food."

Mom had just lit the grill. Gail had brought meat to grill, and there were baking potatoes wrapped in foil to put on the coals. Mom had found all the ingredients for a cold sour cream sauce, and Sophia made a rhubarb pie for dessert. It was a real party meal!

But Dad didn't appreciate any of the food. He complained that he felt sick, and my Mom turned to him with a smile and patted him tenderly on the cheek.

"Poor dear, why don't you go lie down on the sofa for a while?"

Alexandra's mom grinned and made a thumbs up in an "I'm with you, go for it," way at my Mom, almost a little maliciously I thought, because I really did feel sorry that Dad felt so poorly.

"I wonder if Angela has any aspirin?" Dad continued in a suffering tone. "And please, don't grill anything for me, I don't want anything to eat."

Mom looked at him without sympathy and said that he should go and look for aspirin in the medicine cabinet. Dad smiled a pitiful smile, and then went slowly over the lawn and into the house.

"Oh boy, oh boy, oh boy," Alexandra's mom smiled and shook here head. "He does look sick."

"Don't feel sorry for him," Mom said and set the grate right over the glowing coals. "He ate and then danced way too much last night, and now he's paying for it."

I watched Dad as he disappeared through the door into

the house. He hardly ever parties at home, and this is the first time in my life I'd ever seen him so sick. I couldn't help but feel sorry for him, even after what Mom said.

It was a comfort to have everyone here, and it would be a nice cozy evening, in spite of the fact that we had to tell about all the terrible things that had happened to us one more time.

Once again, I had that unreal feeling that everything was a dream even though it had just been a few hours since I'd ridden Fandango at full gallop toward the highway. I could still feel the awful fear in the pit of my stomach. Still, it was like in another world and another time as we sat at the table talking about it. It was obvious that Mom was really upset.

"Are you going to stay here for the night?" she asked Gail who nodded.

"Yeah, I think it's safest."

"We'll stay too," Mom decided. "I'll go home first and get our Labrador retriever, Swift. He's a great watch dog who ..."

Just then, Mom was interrupted by Dad who called pathetically to her. He stood by the house, bent over with his hands on his stomach.

"It hurts so much," he cried, and we all rushed toward him. "I need to go to the hospital …"

"Oh, no," Mom exclaimed anxiously. "What's wrong?"

Dad's face was deathly white and he was sweating rivers. I became ice-cold with fear. What was wrong with him? Was he really that sick?

"I'll call the ambulance," Gail said as she rushed into the house.

"I'll drive him to the emergency room instead," Mom nervously called out. "It's faster!"

But Gail had already disappeared to call.

"Get a lawn chair or something," Mom said as Sophia and I rushed to the nearest one. Dad sank down in the collapsible chair, whimpering with pain, and then he lay entirely still with his eyes closed and his hands clenched in pain.

"What do you think it is?" I asked Mom with a shaking voice. Mom is the district nurse, so she knows a lot about different illnesses.

"Appendix," Gail answered my question coming out of the house. "I bet it's appendicitis. The ambulance is on its way."

Mom crouched down and took Dad's hand. He squeezed her hand weakly back and mumbled something, and tears welled up in my eyes while a big lump formed in my throat.

"Why isn't the ambulance here?" Sophia sniffled and looked at the clock. "Don't they know it's an emergency?" She pushed away a couple of tears that rolled down her cheek, and I knew she was just as scared as I was.

Suddenly we heard sirens in the distance, and soon a huge yellow ambulance turned into the courtyard. Two EMT men came running over with a stretcher and blankets between them. Dad succeeded in getting up and placing himself on the stretcher.

"I'll go with him," Mom said worriedly. "Or would you rather that I stay here?"

"Go with him," Gail said calmly and put her hand on Mom's arm. "The girls and I will be fine. We'll call the police if the tiniest thing happens, I promise."

"Well, if it's okay … then I'll go with him. Promise to call me if anything happens!" Mom said and gave us a worried look. She ran to the ambulance as the EMTs were rolling the stretcher with Dad on it into the ambulance.

I had to swallow a couple of times in order to keep myself from sobbing when the ambulance pulled out of the courtyard and the blue lights went on. The tears burned behind my eyelids and I sniffled. This was just too much!

We had just taken all the food into the kitchen when the phone rang. I answered, and to my surprise it was Officer Roos.

"Hi," he said. "I wanted to tell you that we've been over to the circus and we talked with the circus director. He told us that someone had stolen a clown suit from the costume wagon a few days ago. But he doubted that one of his employees was behind any of this."

"Okay, thanks," I said thoughtfully.

"Is that the police? Sophia mouthed silently and I nodded.

"For the moment I have no further ideas or leads to act on," Andrew continued.

"That's too bad," I said. "Did you talk with anyone else at the circus?" I added and thought about that dark-haired man with the nasty eyes.

"Yeah, a guy called Marko who apparently had a clown act with one of the small horses. Does this jog a memory?"

"Yeah, Angela bought Sunshine from the circus," I said.

"But could it be him? He was very unpleasant when I was there, and seemed angry that Sunshine had been sold."

"He was fully engaged with the circus the whole weekend. Besides, the circus director said that even if Marko has a temper sometimes, he would never do anything that would hurt Sunshine or any horse," Andrew said, and I was sure he'd fully explored that possibility.

All the same, I remembered the impression I had of Marko when Fandango and I were at the circus. There was hatred in his eyes. Well, the circus director and the police may believe what they will, but I was entirely convinced that he was involved in some way!

I hung up and told the others what Andrew had said. We discussed his news for a long time while the August evening, outside the kitchen window, slowly darkened into night. Concern for Dad had given me a knot in my stomach. Mom didn't answer her cell phone, and hadn't called us, either. At half past ten we still didn't know anything about how Dad was doing or what was wrong with him. Gail called the emergency room, but she was told there wasn't a doctor available who had time to speak with her. In any case, the ER nurse said that Dad was lying on the operating table, but she knew nothing else. She asked Gail to call later, which didn't exactly make us less nervous. Poor Dad! We had no idea how he was really doing!

"We ought to take a tour around the farm and make

sure everything is okay before we go to bed," I said in an uncertain voice a moment later.

"That sounds like a good idea," Gail said as she grabbed the large flashlight lying on the shelf.

"Should all four of us go, or …?" Alexandra asked in a fearful voice.

"Of course!" Sophia said with force. "Definitely!"

We carefully locked the house and went around to all the paddocks and pastures to look at the horses. Fandango and Buster were standing quietly, half-asleep in their favorite place – a corner where they could see over almost the entire pasture. They seemed fine.

In the stallion pasture, Bobby, Sunshine and Tuva were calmly grazing. Bobby raised his head and came over to us to see who we were. Then he snorted, disinterested, and returned to his mares and the sweet-tasting grass. In the mare pasture all the foals were lying down asleep while some of their moms watched over them, and the others were grazing.

Everything was calm and peaceful. The fragrance of damp earth lay over the meadows, and when we went into the house again we were wet up to our knees from dew. Both Sophia and Alexandra were freezing, so we decided to have a quick snack and some hot chocolate before going to bed.

Gail said that she would take the easy chair and sit at the top of the stairs to keep watch the whole night, so we could all sleep soundly. It felt safe, but my suspicious mind still worried that she might fall asleep. Since Gail was used to working the night shift she had her knitting and a book with her, so I guessed there was no real danger of her dozing off. We girls drank our hot chocolate and she made herself a little thermos of strong coffee.

We went upstairs. Gail sat down in the easy chair with a blanket and her book, while we three crept into our beds. I lay and read for a while, but after a few minutes I realized I was finding it difficult to get any meaning out of the words I was reading. I reached over, turned off the lamp and had almost fallen asleep when the phone rang and I was immediately wide-awake again.

Both Sophia and I got up and met at the easy chair where Gail sat and talked on the phone.

"How is he?" Sophia whispered, and Gail gave us a thumbs-up.

I felt all the worry melt away, and I took a deep breath. It was as if a heavy weight was lifted from my heart. Then Gail gave me the phone and I heard Mom's voice. She sounded tired but happy.

"Dad had appendicitis," she said. "The doctor told me that he's going to be 100% okay again. He's out of any danger. But how's it going with you girls?"

"Everything is quiet so far," I said. "When's Dad getting out?"

"He'll stay in the hospital for a week, or a little less. They don't know exactly how long it'll be. In a few days you can come visit him."

"Why not tomorrow?" I questioned.

"I don't think he's supposed to have visitors at all tomorrow," Mom said. "The day after an operation a patient usually doesn't feel very well. Please put Sophia on the line. The battery in my cell phone is almost dead!"

I gave the receiver to Sophia and Gail put her arm around my shoulders and gave me a quick hug.

"It must be great to hear that all's well with your Dad before you go to sleep." she said, and I nodded. Strangely enough, I felt almost like crying again, although this time it would be from relief.

I gave a huge yawn, went to my room again and crept into bed. I was asleep before my head had hit the pillow.

Chapter 12

I don't know what it was that woke me, but I think it was that unpleasant feeling I get sometimes when I know I've had a nightmare. I didn't remember what I'd dreamt, but the terror pounded in me still. I reached to turn on the light. But the light wouldn't go on! When I pushed the power breaker, the room was still as dark as before. There was no light on in the hallway where Gail sat. Quickly I sat up in bed, threw off the covers and put my feet on the floor. What was going on?

Just then I heard a deafening rumble and understood at once – it was a thunderstorm!

I got up and tiptoed out to Gail. She stood at the window looking out toward the dark sky and turned toward me.

"Oh, it's only you, Sara," she whispered, and I nodded. "Did the thunder wake you?" she added.

"Yeah," I said. "I think so. Is everything okay?"

"Yes, nothing's happened as far as I can see," Gail said calmly, and I looked out the window to see if I could see anything. "The thunderstorm is coming this way, and our electricity is out."

At that moment, we were blinded by an enormous lightning flash that sparkled across the sky in front of us. Terrified, I froze while Gail calmly counted the seconds.

"There," she said calmly to me. "There's no danger. The thunder is almost six miles away."

"I know," I said in a shaky voice, "but I'm terrified of lightning! And I'm also scared that lightning will hit one of the horses."

"Oh, I see," Gail said. "But it's more likely to hit the windmill over by the highway than anything here on the farm."

"Or the phone pole," I said and gave a backward jump when the next lightning bolt pronged though the sky, followed a moment later by a deafening thunder crash in the distance.

Just then the door to the other room opened and Sophia came out. She gave a big yawn and looked sleepily at us.

"Is it thundering?" she said and then stifled another yawn. "How neat!"

"Neat?" I burst out. "Are you nuts?"

"The air has been so humid for the past few days. After the thunderstorm passes, the air will feel much fresher," Sophia said.

I couldn't understand how she could be so calm, and I thought about how unbelievable it was that we were so different, in spite of the fact that we were sisters, and only two years apart in age. A yawning Sophia stood beside us and looked out the window. Right under the window was the pasture where Bobby hung out with Tuva and Sunshine. Sophia bent over and peered into the darkness. I didn't understand how she could see anything out there, but suddenly she leaned closer to the window with a puzzled look on her face.

"Are there any binoculars here?" she wondered, and Gail gave her Granddad's bird glasses that she'd put on the table beside her chair.

"Do you see something?" I asked.

"I don't know," Sophia said, and pointed the binoculars out through the window. "It's difficult to see when it's so dark. But I thought I saw something moving out there in the pasture …"

"Could it be a horse?" Gail asked in a nervous voice. "Should we call the police?"

"I can't tell for sure," Sophia said and handed the binoculars to me. "Here, Sara. Look and see if you see something. It may be just my imagination. It's so easy to get carried away."

I grabbed the binoculars and pointed it toward the pasture. It was dark. Obviously the moon wasn't out, and the only things I could pick out were Bobby's silver-white spots. He looked like a little pale ghost floating over the grass.

Suddenly I caught a hint of a shadow that appeared to be moving amongst the horses. I tried to stretch my gaze so I'd be able to distinguish moving objects, but all at once everything was still again. Even so, I continued to hold the binoculars on the horses in the pasture. I had a feeling there was something there in the dark even though I couldn't really see it, and I was nervous.

"Can you see anything?" Sophia asked with a shaky

voice, and I shook my head for her to be quiet. She stretched out her hand to take the binoculars, but I pulled them away from her reach.

"Wait your turn!" I hissed.

Just at that moment the sky lit up with another lightning show. For a second the whole world was lit by the chalk-white light, and during that fraction of a second four black shadows appeared – three horses and one person – through my binoculars. And the human shape raised a threatening hand toward one of the horses!

"Call the police," I hissed as the thunder crashed over the fields. "The clown is out there, and I think he's going to kill Sunshine!"

For the next few minutes it seemed like everything was happening in slow motion. Gail grabbed the telephone that was on the table, but naturally it was stone dead because of the storm. I didn't know what to do – run out to the horses or stay inside – so I just stood and looked at Sophia and then Gail and then Sophia again. Sophia looked as terrified and confused as I felt.

"C'mon, let's get out there," she said tensely. "Maybe we can scare him away!"

"No," Gail called out firmly, "you stay here. We don't know how dangerous he is. Don't either of you have a cell phone?"

"Mine's broken," Sophia said. "And Alexandra left hers at home. Sara, do you?"

"I've got mine," I said and rushed into my room and began to search the nightstand in the dark.

My hands were shaking and I had no idea of where it could have gone! I felt everywhere on the small table … cloth … light … book that I was just reading … and clunk went something on the floor! My cell phone!

Quickly I retrieved it, pressed the numbers and the display turned on. What luck that it wasn't broken! Relieved, I hurried out to Gail again. She dialed the number to the police and I went to the window again. It was absolutely pitch black outside. A hard wind shook the trees and made them whistle menacingly. Suddenly there was a loud whispering noise, and the second after it began to rain violently with a clatter on the roof and windowpanes. It poured down, and the big heavy raindrops made so much noise that Gail could hardly make herself heard on the phone.

I peeked out into the dark and tried to see something, but it was hopeless. Sophia tried with the binoculars, but was just as unsuccessful.

My whole body shook as I sank down into the easy chair. It was as if my legs couldn't hold me up any longer! That frightening picture of the dark silhouette that stood with a menacing hand raised toward one of the horses was etched on my retina, and no matter how hard I tried I couldn't get rid of it. It was on constant replay!

Who knew what was happening out there now? Maybe Sunshine was already dead. Or Bobby? Or Tuva – who didn't even belong to Angela but was only here to be bred by Bobby? And what would happen after? Would he leave the other horses in peace, or …? And Fandango?

No, I didn't dare think that thought and I, in total despair, clenched my fists. Things shouldn't be this bad! They should only …

"They're on their way," Gail said as she put the cell phone down. "They said we should stay inside."

"But the horses?" Sophia piped up. "Shouldn't we check on them?"

Gail shook her head.

"We *must* stay inside," she said. It was that light-haired man who was here earlier in the day on the phone."

"That's Officer Roos," I said mechanically.

"Yes, it was he," Gail said trying to sound calm, but I could tell she was just as scared as we were.

The minutes ticked by slowly, slowly. The big clock down in the living room struck two heavy blows at the same moment I looked at the cell phone for the thousandth time.

"Shouldn't they be here? Sophia said yawning. "I'm scared, but I'm also so tired I can hardly stay awake!"

"Go and lie down," Gail said and caressed her cheek. "We'll call you when the police arrive."

"Okay," Sophia said and pattered quietly in to join Alexandra, who was still, incredibly enough, sleeping like a log in their room.

"I'm going to get dressed," I said with a trembling voice. "I'm freezing."

"That's a good idea," Gail said.

I crept into my room and put on a pair of jeans and a thick sweater that I pulled over my nightshirt. I was ice cold and my whole body shook with fear, tension and cold.

When I came out, Gail nodded to me.

"I just saw a pair of car lights," she whispered. "Come on – we'll go down and meet them."

"What about Sophia?"

"She's fast asleep," Gail said. "We can wake her later."

"I'm not sleeping," I heard Sophia's voice from the other bedroom. "I'm coming too!" And she appeared wrapped in a flowery acrylic blanket that Angela used as a bedspread.

We went down the creaking stairs; my mouth was dry from stress and fear. I was so frightened to find out what the clown had done out there … Just thinking about it made my blood freeze! And it didn't get any better when I saw Andrew Roos and Sandy Carson standing in the hallway in their thoroughly wet police uniforms. It was still raining cats and dogs, and every now and then we heard a weak rumble of thunder way off in the distance.

"Tell me what you saw," Andrew said, and I began to tell haltingly about the thunderstorm, binoculars and the horrible scene in the pasture.

"Have you gone out to the horses?" he asked, and both Gail and I shook our heads.

"That's good," he said. "This is what we're going to do. Sandy and I will take our dog and go nose around. If every-thing's calm we'll come back and get you so we can all go together to check on the horses. They may need a vet's care … but we just don't know yet."

Sophia sniffed and Gail put her arm around her shoulders and gave her a calming hug. But I didn't know if she was calming Sophia or herself …

"Lock the door after we go out," Sandy said, and he and Andrew disappeared into the darkness.

"I'm so impressed that they dare," I said, and Gail agreed. Sophia nodded in agreement and yawned. She looked absolutely wiped out, with her hair all messed up and her face gray from exhaustion.

"And yet it is their job," Gail added. "C'mon let's go down to the kitchen. I wish the electricity would come on … I'd give my right arm for a cup of coffee!"

I just stared at her. How could anybody think about coffee in a situation like this? We went down to the kitchen, and I was just about ready to open the refrigerator door and take the milk out when Gail stopped me.

"Wait a bit," she said. "Don't open it unnecessarily. It's better to keep the cold in. We don't know how long the electricity will be off."

"I'm going upstairs and back to bed," Sophia said with a huge yawn. "Will you be sure to come and wake me later?"

"Yes, go back to bed," Gail said in a friendly voice, and Sophia pattered across the floor, dragging the bed cover after her.

I mixed up some powdered drink in a pitcher and Gail set out two glasses. Then we sat in the dark and waited. It was beginning to get light and the dawn promised the beginning of a rainy day. The clouds were heavy over the woods and the rain continued.

Suddenly the electricity snapped on – and the refrigerator hummed.

119

"Finally," Gail said cheerfully as she switched on a light and set up the coffee maker.

I saw the two policemen out in the yard and went to open the door for them.

"Everything appears okay," Sandy said, "but it'll be best if you come with us when we check out the horses. We don't yet have any idea of what he was doing."

I pulled on an old rain jacket that was hanging in the hallway, slipped my feet into my sneakers, and followed the policemen out with Gail on our heels.

It was nasty, raw and cold out. We went quickly to Bobby's pasture and I looked around. I didn't see any horses, and nervously I climbed over the fence.

"Was this the pasture he was in?" asked Andrew, and I nodded and pointed toward the house.

"We were standing up in that window there and looked out."

"Okay," Sandy said calmly. "Well, he's not here now."

"Are you certain about that?" Gail shivered and Andrew nodded.

"Yes, I'm dead certain."

We walked carefully into the pasture and toward a little grove of trees. The grass was sticking to my pant legs and my sneakers got thoroughly soaked. I was shaking with cold and fear and my voice sounded strangely weak when I called for Bobby and Sunshine.

"Maybe they're standing in among the trees," Andrew said calmly, and I nodded mutely.

I had a horrible feeling that everything was going slower

120

than usual. My movements felt heavy, my legs were numb from the cold, my feet were ice cubes, and I was wandering as if in a dream.

"I see them," Andrew suddenly said and pointed. "They're standing over there!"

I followed his finger, and in the next second I yelled out. "No! This can't be happening … it can't be!" As I began to run toward the horses tears flowed down my cheeks. They made me half blind, but it didn't matter, as I knew what it was that I had just seen: Sunshine's golden spots were dark red colored. Dirty red colored – like blood …

Chapter 13

"Paint!" Sophia exclaimed a little later on, smelling her fingertips. "Is he playing with us?"

I set grain out in each of the ponies' grain boxes. My whole body was shaking from shock and fear. It had already been twenty minutes since the police left; Bobby, Sunshine and Tuva stood safely in each of their stalls in the barn. None of the other horses seemed to be hurt in the least, and apparently Sunshine wasn't either. The clown had done nothing more than throw paint all over her! Sticky, gooey red paint now lay in a sheet over her thick mane, back and hindquarters.

"My goodness, how will we ever get her clean?" Sophia said looking at Sunshine. This isn't funny!"

"We can try to scrape as much off as possible," Gail suggested.

"Horse shampoo?" I suggested, but Gail shook her head no.

"We'll start with lukewarm water and see how far we get."

We led Sunshine out of her stall and Gail turned on the water. It was raw and cold and damp out, but with the warm water and the difficult job, we soon warmed up. Gail had gone up to the house and there she met the newly awakened Alexandra who came out to help us.

"It's the tried and true, ever popular barn red color," Gail said drolly, while the color ran off Sunshine in red channels.

I nodded. Dawn was showing its gray light over the courtyard, and I couldn't stop yawning. I felt like I hadn't slept in a hundred years or so!

We finally had most of the color out of her coat. As a finishing touch we washed her two times with horse shampoo, but it didn't seem to make any difference. Sunshine was still red like a barn, but at least her coat felt light and silky smooth. The biggest problem was her mane, which was still clumpy with sticky paint. Sunshine had an incredibly long, thick, golden mane – but right now it seemed like she had long red dreadlocks …

"We'll have to cut her mane," Gail declared. "Will you get the scissors, Sophia?"

"You can't do that!" I huffed. "Angela will go out of her mind and kill us!"

"The most important thing is to get as much of the red paint out as possible." Gail said. "It'll be hopeless getting her clean if she has all her mane left. The mane will grow back again, even if it takes some time."

Swallowing my protest, I nodded in agreement, and then I held Sunshine's head so she would stand still while Sophia cut her mane. It was sad to see the long thick mane fall on the ground, but I knew Gail was right. It would be much easier to wash away the rest of the color once Sunshine was clipped.

"We should call the paint store as soon as it's open and ask if there's anything more we can do," Gail said when we'd finished. Then she yawned. "Now I'm going inside and eating breakfast!" she added.

We put Sunshine in her stall and gave all three ponies some hay. Then we went into the kitchen. Alexandra started to make breakfast. She'd slept the whole night, and she was mad when she heard what she'd missed during the night. I felt like I'd been through a wringer! I hadn't even slept for five hours straight in two nights, and fatigue made my whole body ache. It seemed like my ears were full of gravel, and I wanted to lie down on the kitchen floor right then and fall asleep!

Gail yawned again and muttered something about coffee while Alexandra got the bread, jam and butter.

We ate breakfast, and then Sophia and I went up to bed while Gail and Alexandra decided to keep each other awake. Gail sat down in the armchair outside my room and started knitting. The clinking of the knitting needles sounded safe and cozy, and I felt myself relax and slide into a deep sleep.

Suddenly the telephone rang and, all at once, I was wide-awake again. Gail answered. I heard that it was Angela, and I knew it would be a long conversation. I heard Gail tell her everything that had happened, and after a long time she hung up and looked into my room.

124

"Are you sleeping?" she asked quietly and I sat up in bed.

"No, not yet. Was that Angela?"

Gail nodded.

"Yes, and she had no good news to report. Their truck broke down and they're staying with some folks they know down in Springfield who also raise Shetland ponies. They were towed there a couple of hours ago."

"Oh, no!" I cried. "What's wrong with the truck?"

"Something in the motor broke, and the repair shop in the town they're in doesn't have that spare part. Your Granddad has borrowed a car, and he's on his way to another workshop, about 60 miles from there, to buy the part they need. Then they have to wait for the repair, and that'll take a couple more hours …"

"What'd she say about the clown and everything that happened?" I wondered. "And why didn't they answer their cell phone once over the whole weekend?"

"I didn't ask them about the cell phone," Gail answered. "And about the clown, she has no idea, just like us. She said she has no idea who it could be either, as she's never met a clown or anyone who would want to hurt her or the ponies. But she'll call the police and speak with them when she gets back."

"That's good," I said and lay down again. "Oh, but I'm tired," I added. "Is Sophia sleeping?"

"Yeah, she's snoring anyway!" Alexandra said, peeking through the door behind her mom.

"Well, I guess we have to stay here until they come home," I said doubtfully.

"Yes, but unfortunately I can't stay because I need to work at the hospital tonight," Gail said. "And I won't let Alexandra stay here, either," she added.

I nodded.

"Mom can probably come," I said. "But Dad's in the hospital ..."

"Yes, but she can come and bring Swift with her," Gail said. "I'll call her to make sure. If she can't stay with you, we'll have to arrange something else, because you and Sophia absolutely can't stay here alone. It's altogether too dangerous. We have no idea what that crazy person will do next."

I nodded and gulped. It seemed more horrible when Gail said it out loud, even though I already knew it. Anything could happen, and fear set in my stomach like a hard knot when I lay down again, closed my eyes and tried to sleep.

I slept for a few hours, with uneasy dreams about thunderstorms, lightning and being chased, but I couldn't run away because my body was so slow and heavy.

When I woke, it was afternoon. I was wet with sweat and the sheet was entirely twisted up in the bed. Although I was still groggy, I got up and went down to the kitchen where Gail, Alexandra and Sophia were playing *Hearts*.

"Mike is coming over in a while," Gail said when I plopped down at the kitchen table. He'll stay here tonight, and your Mom's coming over in about an hour and a half. She's at the hospital and she'll drive directly here."

"Mike is going to be staying here – with me?" I asked, surprised.

"Yeah, and Alexandra and I are going with Gail," Sophia said, and I stared at her.

"Just great!" I exploded in a rage. "Why do you get to go home?"

Sophia shrugged her shoulders.

"I have a lot to do," she said. "You, Mike and Mom will be fine without me!"

"Yeah, I'm sure we will," I hissed with anger. "You … deserter."

"Why am I a deserter?" Sophia burst out. "I have something better to do than watch Granddad and Angela's horses! It's one thing for you to be here – you're interested in horses. I said from the beginning that I'd stay here until today, but I can't for the life of me think about staying a minute longer than I have to."

"It isn't about that," I said with anger. "You're just afraid that something will happen, and …"

"Stop fighting now," Gail said and put up a warning hand. "No one has to stay here unless they want to. You can go home too if you want, Sara. Your Mom and Mike can certainly manage without you."

"I'll stay," I exhaled irately.

"There, you see," Sophia said snottily. "I do what I want, and you do what you want!"

I stared at her with hatred. Sometimes she was just too much!

After we cleaned up the kitchen and loaded all their baggage in the car, I went over to the barn and took Sunshine out on a lead rope. Tuva and Bobby were in their pasture. It was cloudy and the air was stuffy and humid, in spite of the night's thunderstorm. I shivered. It didn't feel comfortable to be by myself in the barn, but I was so angry with Sophia that I couldn't bear to stay in the house with her any longer.

Carefully, I looked around. I tried to put the clown and everything associated with him out of my mind, but that was impossible.

A puff of wind through the lilac bushes made me jump, and when I heard a car motor in the distance, I felt my heart beat thump, thump, thump. But then I saw the car, and a warm feeling of security spread over me. I smiled broadly as I watched Mike park and get out of the car.

"Finally!" I shouted and rushed forward to give him a hug, but before I could throw my arms around him, he took me by the shoulders and held me at a distance.

"Stop! I don't want red paint on my clothes!" he grinned in a teasing way and I just sighed.

"The spots are from last night. They're already dry! Besides, I didn't know you were such a clothes snob," I said smiling, and Mike pulled me toward him.

"I could be," he mumbled with his lips near my ear. "But it's okay for this time only."

Then he gave me a big hug, and I felt the relaxation spread over me now that he was here. "Wonderful, my beloved Mike … Now everything'll be okay!"

Mike let Swift out of the back of his car and then we went down to the pasture to look at Sunshine.

"What happened, really?" he asked while we stood in

the pasture and patted the three ponies who had come over to us filled with curiosity. "Your Mom told a long and involved story about a crazy clown who's caused a bunch of trouble. Is he the one who put the red paint on Sunshine?" he asked, and I nodded.

"Yes, he was," I said and sucked in a deep breath. "But it really started when I rode Fandango over here the other day …"

It took a good long time for me to repeat the whole story, and when I finished Mike looked really concerned.

"It sounds so weird," he said, shaking his head. "I can see why you're so upset!"

"Yes, and even worse than that is the fact that we've called the police, several times, and they've done almost nothing! They could at least have a police car standing by, for example, trying to catch the clown in the act."

"It isn't that easy," Mike said as we walked slowly toward the house. "They have a bunch of other things to do."

"I know," I said, yawning a huge yawn, "but still … For Pete's sake, we were scared, especially the first night before Gail arrived."

When we got to the house the others were ready to go. Sophia refused to look at me, but I didn't have the energy to be angry with her any longer. I just wanted to be together with Mike and Mom.

After Mike and I had waved good-bye to them, I began to yawn again and Mike told me to go take a nap.

"I promise to keep watch and make sure nothing happens," he said. "Go up, and sleep well."

"Are you sure?" I yawned again, and Mike pecked me on the cheek.

"Of course. I'll wake you if something happens. Your Mom ought to be here any time.

I tripped up the stairs, lay down on my bed and fell asleep at once. I don't think it even took a minute before ...

Chapter 13

I awoke at almost 4:30 PM. I had slept almost five hours, but it still wasn't enough for me to be fully functioning and cooking on all four burners, but I got up anyway and found Mike in the kitchen making food. Mom sat at the kitchen table reading the evening paper, and dinner smelled heavenly.

"There was some meat in the freezer," he said. "I also found some leftover French-fries. Are you hungry?"

"Yes," I nearly shouted. "Starved! I haven't eaten since six this morning. How's Dad?" I asked anxiously, and Mom looked up.

"Much better!" she said. "He has some pain after the operation, of course, but we hope he can come home on Thursday or Friday."

I pulled out a kitchen chair, sat down and browsed a little through the evening paper's extra sections. After a few minutes it was time to eat, which we three did with hearty appetites.

After the meal, Mike and I went out to bring Fandango

and Buster in. It had rained a while during the afternoon, and they stood waiting at the gate. Buster didn't usually care about the cold, but I absolutely didn't want Fandango to stay out when he was cold and wet.

I felt so much safer when Mom, Mike and Swift were in the yard with me. Swift nosed around the farm happily, wagged his tail, and looked exactly how a fat, satisfied, friendly Labrador should look. But I knew if something really bad happened he could bark deafeningly, growl angrily, and act like a really dangerous attack dog.

Fandango and Buster followed nicely and went into their stalls, and I gave them each a little hay. Then I stood and made a fuss over Fandango – and suddenly I decided to go for a ride. Mike was a little anxious until I said that I would only ride in the pasture closest to the barn, which he agreed sounded safe.

"We really have to train more," I said while brushing Fandango. "We haven't done much training over the past few days, with everything else going on!"

But in spite of the fact that I was so certain I wanted to ride, my stomach felt queasy as we entered the pasture. It was hard to not sneak glances at the huge bushes, and even though I rode a long way from them, I found that I couldn't focus on my riding!

Mike had come with us. He stood and watched with critical glances, but didn't say anything.

"Yikes, that wasn't good," I said as I rode over to him and made a face. "I can't concentrate."

"I can see that," Mike said. "Do you want me to help?"

"Yes, please," I said with a little doubt. "Although it's not of any value unless …"

"You give up too easily," Mike said and winked at me. Then he suggested different walking and trotting exercises. No real difficult ones, but since he demanded that we did everything perfectly, Fandango and I were forced to concentrate on the commands. In time, things went much better, and when Fandango did his absolute best in a calm, steady trot with rein commands only, I thought that it wasn't so bad after all to train for dressage. If only Dad would stop being so bossy the whole time!

We took Fandango in and Mike waited while I cooled him down. It had begun to blow more, and it felt like autumn was already here. I shivered in my thin sweater and we hurried into the house.

I showered and changed into the clean clothes that Mom had brought, and then I sat down in the living room with Mom and Mike. It was almost seven o'clock, and the wind rustled through the trees outside the living room window. Mike and I sat on the sofa, and I covered myself with a warm, cozy blanket. We drank tea and made small talk while we watched TV. Everything was peaceful, Mike had his arm around my shoulders, and Mimi came and lay down with me on the sofa. She purred in a peaceful way, and it seemed like she was watching TV too – although she wasn't because when I leaned forward and looked at her face, her eyes were closed!

About half past eleven, I began to feel that it was time for bed and a good night's sleep. Mike and Mom had promised to stay awake and keep watch during the night so I'd be able to sleep.

"I bet you'll fall asleep immediately," Mike said, grinning in a teasing way at my attempts to keep my eyes open.

I yawned a huge yawn and began to separate myself from the blanket to go and lie down in my bed instead.

Mike had just turned off all the lights downstairs and I had almost reached the top stair when we heard a high-pitched whinny. Even though I was half asleep, my heart began to pound like a sledgehammer and my senses were on high alert as I stood entirely still on the top step.

"Did you hear a horse neigh?" Mike whispered from the downstairs hallway. "Or am I imagining it?"

"No, I heard it too," I nervously whispered. "Oh no, I hope it's not him again … I can't stand any more of this!"

"Now, now," Mom said trying to sound calm, but I could hear in her voice how anxious she was. "It doesn't have to be the clown. Horses whinny every now and then. There's nothing strange about that."

"It's him," I exploded, and felt my fear blend with my hatred for him. "I know it's him! And I hate him … hate!"

"Do you have your cell phone upstairs?" Mike asked as he ran quickly and quietly up the stairs. While he dialed the number to the police, I sneaked over to the window and looked out from behind the curtain. A small spotlight over the barn door lit up the courtyard, but I couldn't see anything moving.

Just then I heard another whinny and I saw a tiny black shadow sneak forward quickly along the lit barn wall. The black shadow went in through the barn door that stood slightly open, and then he disappeared into the barn's darkness. I swallowed and blinked because I wanted to be sure that I had seen right. What was he doing in the barn? There aren't any horses in there. I was confused, and scanned the area to try to see if anything else was happening. Bobby and the mares were out in the pasture, like all the other Shetland ponies ...

At that same second, my tired brain woke up and I remembered that, of course, there were horses in there – Buster and *Fandango*! My darling pony was in that dark barn – with a crazy man who could be doing anything!

I stared with tears stinging my eyes while I listened to Mike talk with the police. How could he be so calm and levelheaded? I couldn't understand it!

One second later the barn door swung wide open, and I could hear hooves tapping. I could see a dark shadow against the lit barn door, and a gray horse!

Fandango!

My fear suddenly turned into burning fury, and I roared, "No!" It was like everything just burst open within me! Fueled by fury, I rushed out of the room, down the stairs, and right out into the August night. I heard Mom scream something to me, but I didn't listen. I just ran as fast as I could! Now, after it's all over, I don't understand how I ever dared – but one thing's for sure – I was so fueled by anger and hatred that all fear and self-preservation were pushed aside.

The clown wouldn't have a chance to do anything bad to

Fandango – that I would make sure of! The dew-wet grass felt icy cold on my bare feet, but there was no relief going from the grass to the barnyard's sharp gravel. I saw the dark shadow get up on Fandango who, in confusion, stood stock still without any sense of what was about to happen.

"Leave my horse alone!" I screamed, with all the anger I could muster. "Let him go!" I rushed forward and took hold of the bridle on Fandango's right side while at the same time I tried to push the black shadow from his back. Since I had appeared so unexpectedly, I managed for a moment to get the intruder off balance, but just as I started to push him off, he kicked me with his big foot. The large clown shoe hit me in the chest, and even though it didn't particularly hurt it made me lose my balance. I staggered a bit and stepped on a sharp rock. It hurt so much that I shrieked at full blast, but in spite of the pain I had one single thought in my head – that I would not let go of Fandango's bridle. If I did that, then the repulsive clown would do something bad to Fandango after he had disappeared into the dark with my beloved horse! And I wasn't going to let that happen!

Without knowing what to do, I pulled Fandango in a little circle around me.

The man on his back twisted and grabbed the reins, and at the same time he kicked toward me with his foot and swore a long, nasty string of words. Suddenly a hand came toward me as he tried to hit me! I was able to duck, but I felt his fingertips graze my head.

"No," I puffed. "You can't have him. Let go of my horse! Let go of the reins!"

I was breathless, and I could hardly talk, let alone try to sound authoritative or fearless, but even just saying the words helped me keep fighting.

The seconds seemed eternally long. We turned around and around in the dirt. My feet were numb from pain and cold, and I wondered, in my confusion, what Mike was doing. Why didn't he come to help me? For heavens sake, where was he? This whole thing was like one of those bad dreams where I never know or understand what's happening – but even though I'm terribly confused, I know I absolutely must not give up …

Fandango naturally didn't understand what was happening, and he became more difficult to hold. Suddenly he raised up his back leg and kicked sideways at me. I slipped away like a hand out of a mitten and landed on my back in the gravel, and then I heard Fandango's hooves thunder away from the courtyard.

My first thought was that I'd failed – that the clown had ridden away on my horse! – But then I heard someone yell and noticed that a fight was going on right beside me. Pushing, pounding and enraged swearwords were exchanged between two figures in the dark.

"Mike," I sniffled, and confusion blended with relief.

I must help him, I thought, and I limped toward the two who were fighting even though I could hardly be of much help because of the condition I was in.

All at once the farm's huge spotlights flashed on. You could only turn them on from the house, and in the blinking light I saw Mom come running from the house. She must have turned on the lights, I thought, and at the same time I saw Mike come running after her. I was confused as I couldn't understand how Mike could be both on the way to the yard and at the same time fighting with the disgusting clown in the yard. It was like my brain wasn't registering what was happening. I just stood quietly with my arms hanging and stared at the fight, and then at Mom and Mike who came rushing over.

When the spotlight blinked again and finally began to light up at full strength I got the biggest surprise of my life! In front of me in the chalk-white light the clown had fallen on the ground with one arm bent behind his back. On the clown's back was a person dressed in black who had a cruel but satisfied smile on his face – Marko! It was Marko who had fought the clown and saved Fandango.

But then who was the clown?

Chapter 14

Several hours later, around mid morning, we all sat in Angela and Granddad's kitchen – we meaning Mom, Gail, Mike, the circus director, Angela, Granddad, Andrew Roos and me. Andrew sat on the kitchen sofa with a cup of coffee, and suddenly there were steps in the hall. Marko, Alexandra and Sophia came in, each carrying a plastic lawn chair from the garden. Gail had picked up Alexandra and my sister on her way home from her night job at the hospital so they all could come over to hear the latest. They then went out to the pasture together with Marko to say hello to Sunshine. They stayed there for a really long time, I thought, glancing at the kitchen clock again. Suspiciously long! And my little sister certainly looked more than a little rosy red in the cheeks when she sneaked a look at Marko …

"What a story," Mom said shaking her head. "You always seem to be in the middle of some odd mystery, Sara!"

"It's not like I ask for it – it just happens to me," I said wearily.

"Besides, Alexandra and I were here too," Sophia said –

avoiding the whole issue of going home like a coward the day before, instead of staying at the farm until Granddad and Angela came home.

The coffee maker gurgled and the aroma spread over the kitchen. Angela set out bread, butter and cheese while Granddad served up the coffee.

"Oh, my," Angela said, sinking down on the kitchen sofa. "What a weekend this has been!"

"Yes, I can easily second that," I said. "Anyway, how'd the show go?"

"Spotty won his class and received great points, and the little stallion was the young stallion champion, and he came in third in the best-in-show," Angela said with pleasure as she laid out the big colorful ribbons on the table.

"But why didn't you call us at once and tell us what had happened?" she continued, looking first at me and then at Sophia. "We would've come directly home if we'd known!"

"We tried to call," Sophia said, "but your cell phone was turned off the whole time. If you listen to your messages you'll hear at least a hundred from us!"

Angela looked at Granddad with a frown. Granddad looked at the floor and turned red.

"Hmmm, the cell phone," he said. "Yes, it was lying in the glove compartment the whole weekend. Neither the old woman nor I are particularly into the new technologies."

"Tell us everything one more time, from the very beginning," Angela said while Granddad served her more coffee and Mom cut up thick slices of bread.

140

Sophia, Alexandra and I all started at once to tell the story – but this time I knew the progression didn't seem correct. And it wasn't really the whole story – so now Marko and the circus director helped, at last, to tell the ending – and, most importantly, to answer the persistent question of "why?"

"I guess it started on the same day I found Fandango at the circus," Marko said.

He put four sugar cubes in his coffee cup and stirred them around before he continued.

"I had argued with Nick, one of the guys who works as a jack-of-all trades at the circus. I never liked him. He's often mean to the horses and, I'd warned him a number of times to stop what he was doing or he'd be out of a job.

Marko took a slurp of coffee.

"I had been dating one of the girls in the acrobat group," he continued. "When we broke up several months ago, she and Nick started going out. It didn't bother me, since our relationship had ended, and … Eloise and I stayed good friends. But about a week ago, she came to me and said that sometimes Nick was so drunk that he hit her. I got really angry when I heard that. I said to her that she should end her relationship with Nick, and I invited her to stay in my trailer until she could find something else. I would sleep at my parents' who had an extra bed in their trailer."

The circus director gave a deep sigh.

"I don't know why I wasn't able to see through Nick," he said, pressing his index finger into the breadcrumbs on the

141

tablecloth. "I don't get it … I'd always thought he seemed like an exceptionally stable and fine young man!"

"He's good at fooling people," Marko said calmly. "It's his strong suit."

"That type of person often makes a good impression, unfortunately," Andrew interjected, and then Marko continued with his story.

"The same morning that you showed up at the circus, Nick and I had a terrible argument. Nick was, to put it politely, really peeved at me, and when you spoke with the director and me about Sunshine, he suddenly figured out a way to get revenge. He knew that I wasn't happy that Sunshine had been sold. If he could just get you to believe that I was the one making all the problems for you, then I'd be in trouble."

"I see!" Sophia burst out. "That's the reason why!"

"And then what?" I said irritably, because I wanted to hear the end of the story – and not my little sister's uninteresting theories about different things.

"He probably figured out that Sunshine didn't belong to us, and that Angela, the real owner, wasn't home," Sophia continued, pretending she didn't hear the irritation in my voice.

"That's true," Alexandra said, "We thought it was so strange that someone would try to scare us. We were only visiting, and Sunshine and the others aren't even our horses."

"I don't know if he thought that through," Marko said. "He was quite simply only after me. It was pure luck that I began to suspect Nick was behind the pranks at your farm.

When my clown suit was stolen and the police came to the circus and asked some strange questions, I simply put two and two together."

Marko drank the last of his coffee and Granddad got up to refill the coffee maker for the third time.

"I wanted to follow Nick directly here the night before last, but he sneaked away without my noticing that he was gone. When I finally got here, the damage was already done and you were just taking Sunshine and the others in."

"That was terrible! We thought that he'd stabbed her with a knife all over her body!" Sophia said, and reddened. Marko nodded.

"At first I thought that too, but then I found a can with red paint and a pair of white paint-stained gloves lying in a bag outside the fence, and then I knew that it wasn't what I thought it was. I went to the police, and I was absolutely sure they'd know it belonged to Nick."

"You mean because there'd be finger prints?" Sophia asked, and Marko nodded.

"Maybe, or maybe not. It's difficult to guess. A pair of white gloves is common and can be bought in just about any store, but I should be able to find the store where he bought them. Besides, Nick is no real clown. He just dresses as one when he leads the ponies around for the pony rides."

"Exactly, I remember the pony rides …" I mumbled almost inaudibly, and suddenly remembered the smiling clown who came over to us with the little black and white pony on a lead rope when we stood and chatted at the water faucet.

I reddened and wondered to myself if Nick had already begun to make plans about creating trouble for us.

"Ooooh, think about how he tried to chase the ponies onto the highway," I said with a shudder. "That was horrible!"

Andrew nodded slowly.

"Yeah, he was setting up a dangerous accident," he said. "It wasn't just the ponies that would have been seriously injured or even killed. A whole lot of innocent motorists were at risk, too. I don't know for sure, but my guess is he'll go to jail for a long time."

"Don't forget those dreadful postcards, too," Alexandra said. "Especially after we knew he'd been in the house … we were scared to death!"

"I know," Mom said. "We never would have let you be here alone if we'd known all this would happen!"

"Oh don't make such a big fuss, it wasn't really that dangerous!" Sophia said trying to sound tough.

"Really?" I said and raised my eyebrows to show my disbelief. "You were just as scared as we were, as I recall …"

"Yes, but … Well!" Sophia said with a red face, and then she sat quietly and let Marko finish telling the story.

"There was no evening performance yesterday, so I could watch Nick constantly without being disturbed. At about 11:30 PM he left and I followed him here. After we got here I wasn't sure what he planned to do, so I followed him around. I was lucky that it was dark and he couldn't see me as he bridled the gray horse and led it out of the barn and hopped on."

"And then I came running out!" I interrupted. "I grabbed

hold of Fandango's bridle and tried to push him off his back."

"And I was trying to pull him off from my side, but then you began to turn the horse around in tight circles and I lost my grip. But I knew that sooner or later he'd fall off – Nick can't ride very well, and sitting on a horse bareback isn't the easiest thing."

"What do you think he was going to do with Fandango?" I asked, and Marko shrugged his shoulders.

"I don't know, and I honestly believe he didn't either. I think he was going to ride around a little, and he hoped you would see him eventually from the window. He certainly knew that you kept watch at night, but maybe he thought he had time to get away before you could come out. He'd done it every night before. He finally fell off and tried to run away, but I got hold of him, and ... well, the rest you know. The police came and we hope he's behind bars ..."

"Of course he is," Andrew said, and I tried to stifle a yawn. "You can sleep peacefully at night again."

"Thanks and Hallelujah for that," Angela said with a yawn too. "We slept in the truck for four nights, and I will only say one thing – the next time we stay in a hotel!"

"But that'll be too expensive," Granddad grumbled. Angela stared quietly at him, and I knew that if Granddad planned to sleep in the truck for a few days, he'd be sleeping there alone!

"How great that we got everything in order for you, anyway," Mom said relaxing.

"Yeah, and what luck you weren't mad that we cut off

Sunshine's mane," I said, and grinned at Angela while she made a frown

"I know it was necessary," she sighed, "but couldn't you have saved a little bit, at least?"

"No," Sophia and I said in unison.

"We couldn't," added Sophia. "You should've seen how she looked!"

"But I'll give you my allowance if you want to buy a wig for her," I joked. "I'm sure we can find one on the Internet."

"Hmmm," Angela grinned. "I'm not crazy about the idea, but thanks anyway!"

A few hours later we were finally on our way home. Fandango and I got a ride from Granddad who borrowed a horse trailer from a neighbor. Guess how great that felt not to have to ride all the way home! I sat and dozed in the front seat, hardly saying a word the whole way, but Granddad babbled happily on about the show, the clown, the broken truck and a bunch of other stuff.

When we finally got home Fandango seemed happy to see Camigo and Maverick again. He rushed into the pasture at a quick gallop with his tail straight up, snorting like a steam engine. Then he stopped at the pasture's dustiest place, bent his legs, and rolled side to side with pleasure for a long time. I stood and watched him, yawned my hundredth yawn, and decided not to ride at all that day.

Mike had gone to his house, Mom had started the wash, and I went up to my room and turned on the computer. I was too tired to do anything that required much work, but too awake to sleep, so I decided to write an e-mail to my best friend, Jessie, and tell her everything that had happened. When I logged on to the Internet, the little envelope was blinking – which means I'd gotten e-mail over the weekend. It was from Fiona, which woke me up immediately. My heart pounded as I quickly read the two-day old note:

Hi Sara!
Winny just left. The vet checked her out, and I'll send you all her papers by snail mail. The horse transport said that she should arrive at your place about noon on Tuesday. Please answer this letter and let me know that you got it, and that you'll be home when Winny arrives!
Good luck with Winny! I hope you have a wonderful life together. She is a terrific horse, even if she and I didn't really click.
C U Soon,
Fiona

I stood up from my desk so fast that I almost went over backwards. I rushed downstairs and ran into Mom who'd just come out of the laundry room with her arms full of clean clothes.

"What's the matter?" she asked anxiously. "Has something happened?"

"Yeah," I was overjoyed. "Winny is on her way … and she'll be here in an hour and a half!"

Chapter 15

Sophia came in my room all wild-eyed with excitement.

"What's with you?" I asked, and Sophia blushed totally red.

"I got an e-mail from Marko a while ago! He's coming here to say hi when the circus finishes for the summer."

"Hello!" I exploded. "He's gotta be way too old for you!"

"I'm almost fifteen, and he is only *just* 18," Sophia said confidently. "Besides, he's the sweetest-cutest-nicest guy I have ever met!"

"You said that about Alexandra's brother, too," I said. "*And* about his friend with the dark hair … and about that sports fanatic who wanted you to jog and do aerobics with him!"

"Cut it out, Sara," Sophia said and rolled here eyes. "This thing with Marko is different! Just think how romantic … we can maybe live in his trailer some day and go around with the circus. And I could get a job there, and maybe even have my own act …"

I stared at my sister, and for a moment I had a vision of how she would look, tripping around in the sawdust like a circus monkey with a fluffy tutu and a little umbrella in her hand. And then I imagined her future as a circus princess – that certainly fits my little sister like a glove – maybe a clown's white glove!